REVIEWS

"By empathising with the tumult that accompanies growing up and injecting the right amounts of peril, fantasy and realism, whilst also keeping the language colloquial and un-cluttered, Alan Stephenson has constructed a character that could capture the imagination of the elusive teen audience." - **Galway Independent**

" [Stephenson]makes an entertaining emulsion of rhythm, danger, character empathy and the usual teenage dilemmas of getting to grips with hormones and emergent adulthood.

Tolkien and JK Rowling built empires out of this blueprint. If Stephenson can build on this debut and bring further riches to what he intends to be a trilogy, who knows where this could lead." - **Hilary A. White, Irish Independent**

"The book features more than just excellent pacing; Gabby shows extraordinary, inspiring courage as she comes to terms with being suddenly alone in the world." - **Gerrit Nuckton, Connemara Journal**

Gabby
A Mythical Journey

Alan Stephenson

Copyright

This book is copyright material and must not be copied, reproduced, transferred, distributed, leased, licensed or publically performed or used in any way except as specifically permitted in writing by the publishers, as allowed under the terms and conditions under which it was purchased or as strictly permitted by applicable copyright law. Any unauthorised distribution or use of this text may be a direct infringement of the author's and publisher's rights and those responsible may be liable in law accordingly.

Version 2.0

www.agirlnamedgabby.com

Gabby a Mythical Journey Copyright © 2015 Alan Stephenson

All rights reserved.

ISBN: 1515383962
ISBN-13: 978-1515383963

Alan Stephenson has asserted his right under Copyright and Related Rights Act, 2000 to be identified as the author of this work.

This novel is a work of fiction, Names and characters are a product of the author's imagination and any resemblance to actual persons, living or dead, is entirely coincidental.

First published in Ireland in 2014 by Lettertec Irl. Ltd. Springhill House, Carrigtwohill, Co. Cork, Ireland.

ISBN 9781910098229

Cover by Cuán Mara Design

ACKNOWLEDGEMENTS

I'd like to thank my editor, Jean Mullan and her husband Pat, for their invaluable help and friendship. I'd like to thank my family for their encouragement, but most of all I'd like to thank my sister Jane for being such a positive part of my life.

Chapter 1

She was incredibly patient. She had been stalking the crab for more than twenty minutes now, all the way alongside the breaking waves, her fur matted and drenched by the sea. Sophie didn't mind getting wet. It was all for a good cause. She reached her launch area about four feet away from the intended target, pounced high into the air, landing full tilt on the tiny creature, grabbing it in her front paws and trying hard to pull out the occupant. Alas, it was all to no avail and so she did what most cats would do in similar situations; she feigned disinterest.

The hermit crab was being battered back and forth at the water's edge, not by the tide, but by the cat's furry paw. The beautiful half-Persian animal belonged to the girl sitting atop the small sand dune a few yards away.

'Sophie! Stop it! Leave the poor creature alone!' said the girl, with laughter in her voice. The magnificent cat turned and ran toward the girl, its long hair blowing like the white tufts of bog cotton in the windy fields of western Connemara.

Gabriella sat in the same place every night. She made a point of watching the sun set because all her short life she'd been told 'Death' was just around the corner. So intent was her focus on catching the last glimpse of the sun setting over the Atlantic Ocean that she didn't notice her best friend stalking her from behind.

Sophie tried hard to leap up onto Gabby's shoulder but the softer sand of the dune put an undignified end to that plan. Her little head crashed unceremoniously into the girl's back.

'What are you at, you little monkey?' she asked, reaching behind and picking up her ball of fluff. Sophie loved the attention she received from her owner and became a dead weight in the girl's hands. Gabby laid her down on a towel on top of her raised legs, tummy up.

'You should have been an otter, you're soaked,' she said drying the cat's tummy. Sophie grabbed the towel and hands with all fours but didn't scratch her mistress. She never did.

With her elegant young fingers she scratched under the furry chin and unmatted the long unruly hair. As the grooming continued, the cat's head was bent over Gabby's knees, making her world upside down. She purred ecstatically as she watched the little crab scurry back into the sea.

Gabby stood, playfully tossing the cat onto the sand while watching the deepening darkness descend toward the distant horizon.

'Come on you, tea time!' she said running down the far side of the dune and then up toward her home, Sophie chasing behind all the way.

CHAPTER 2

Gabby was drying her long hair as she exited the tiny bathroom. It was no easy chore washing it in such cramped conditions even once a week. Her grandfather had rigged a hot water system outside but there was still never enough to supply the needs of her and her mother. The mobile home on the other hand was quite big; they each had a full-sized bed that didn't need to be assembled every night.

Gabriella Caitlan O'Toole would be fifteen for two more hours. She was so excited about the 'coming of age' party her family were throwing for her the following night. She sat down at her mother's dressing table trying hard to untangle her hair.

'You know, Mama, we should just cut it all off. It would be so much easier, don't you think?' Caitlan, Gabby's mother, approached the dressing table, brush in hand.

'Much easier dear, let's do it.' She pulled a large pair of gardening shears from behind her back.

'Hold still now.'

'Mama no! Stop!'

Gabby shrieked bending forward in mock hysteria, part of their weekly ritual. Caitlan put down the shears and turned back to her smiling daughter, gently stroking out the long wavy strands of brilliant red hair.

She studied Gabby's face as she had many, many times before. Her skin was light olive, freckles around her nose, iridescent green eyes and the hair of course. All the elegance and beauty of her daughter was hers except the olive skin. That was her father's.

Caitlan had had the same hair until that day sixteen years ago. Overnight it had changed colour to the purest white. Some people she'd come across since mistook her for an albino, but she wasn't. The shock and brutality of *the incident* had caused the change, the doctor insisted. Didn't matter to her now, she had grown to love her hair as much as she loved her daughter.

After the festivities on the following- night, the camp would be struck once more. The family only stayed in one place for two months at the most. Security had been ingrained in all of them since Gabriella's birth. They travelled the length and breadth of Ireland and only at night, for safety reasons.

'Mama, what's going to happen tomorrow, to me?' Caitlan looked into her innocent eyes and replied,

'We don't know darling, maybe nothing. It might all just be a myth, so don't fret yourself.'

She wrapped her arms around Gabby's neck.

'Besides, we'll be here to protect you.'

She finished combing out the long tresses of her daughter's hair, a job she loved to do. Gabby stood and turned to hug her mother.

'I'm glad you're here, Mama. I love you.' She kissed her cheek and walked toward her bed.

'Will you be warm enough?' Caitlan asked frowning at Gabby's boxer shorts and flimsy T-shirt. Gabby leapt onto the bed pulling the covers up to her head.

'Yes Mama, as always, I will be fine.' Caitlan bent down

and kissed her daughter's head.

'Sleep well sweetheart. Love you.'

'Love you too.'

The explosion was so intense at the far end of the caravan that the concussion blew out the long Plexiglass window beside her bed, causing it to land some ten feet away with Gabby on top of it. The noise of the fire consuming her home of fifteen years mixed with gunfire and screams terrified her, but not enough to stop her running back inside.

'Mama! Mama! Where are you? Mama!' she screamed.

The acrid smoke and flames didn't seem to affect her much as she reached her mother's burning bed. She felt for a body but there was nothing.

'Mama?' she screamed once more. Then, by carefully listening she picked up the faintest sound of someone in severe pain coming from the tiny bathroom. The flames licked at her ankles and legs but she felt nothing as she threw open the bathroom door. Her mother was sitting on the commode, her skin badly burned and her hair and nightdress on fire.

'Mama! Oh Mama, no, no!'

She fearlessly lifted her mother into her arms and charged back outside rolling on the damp ground to extinguish the flames. Gabby cradled her mother's head.

'Mama? Mama?'

Through her burned and parched lips her young mother croaked, 'Gabby, oh Gabby, you must run . . . to Mo Mo's island, you're not safe now . . . they've found you.'

Tears spilled down their faces; they had both known this day might come.

Gabby started to argue but the sound of more gunfire erupted around them. She began to lift her mother's damaged body but before it left the ground a bullet singed her outer ear and struck her mother's chest. Her eyes opened with steely determination.

'Gabriella, Mo Mo will teach you all . . . leave me . . . be safe darling . . . I . . . love . . . you . . . .' She passed into unconsciousness.

Gabby looked around and spotted Sophie, tail on fire, bolting toward the sea.

'Run baby run!!' she screamed, knowing she could do nothing for her cat, there were more important things to do. All four of her family's caravans were either ablaze or blown apart. She wiped her eyes. The smouldering bodies of her family lay all around.

Bullets continued to ping around her as she surveyed the damage. She knew she had to run from this place in order to live. She could see the muzzle flashes high up on the cliffs, two, four, maybe five she counted, too many for her to fight. So she ran and ran.

CHAPTER 3

She felt nothing but heartache and loneliness as she ploughed into a thicket of brambles half a mile away from the awful destruction. She saw flashing blue lights crawling like beetles over the hills from every direction.

Gabby presumed every one she knew was dead, except Mo Mo Kelly whom she'd met years ago but she didn't really *know* at all. They had drilled into her since she was a little girl that bad people were looking for her and would continue their search until she was dead.

This is no good! she thought to herself as she moved on through the prickly gorse bushes that are common in the west of Ireland. They pulled at her shorts and T-shirt trying to ensnare her like a spider in its web.

Her Mama had said that the little fishing villages of Cleggan or Derryinver would best suit her for stealing a small dinghy or currach in which to get to Kelly's Island.

The wise elders of the gypsy clan of which she was a member had told her she might inherit the most unusual powers known to man, tomorrow, on her sixteenth birthday. She deduced this was why such a concerted effort had been made to kill her earlier. It would be their last chance and now they had failed. Gabby would make them pay dearly for that mistake.

She estimated it must be around midnight by now but nothing seemed to have changed. *Where are my super powers?* she asked herself. So, on she walked into the night, ripping her shirt and legs occasionally on unseen thorns. There was no pain but she imagined come daylight there would be some nasty cuts. After an hour she spotted 'the grandmother of trees' as her mum would call it: a towering eight hundred year old oak on the hill off to her right backlit by a partially cloud-covered moon.

Gabby decided the prudent thing to do was to climb high into the gnarled limbs in case anybody was following. She'd been up in the tree many times over the years but always during daylight hours. She reasoned to herself it was worth taking the risk of slipping from a branch to ensure her safety from men with guns. So up she went.

She reached a spot where a large bough joined the main trunk roughly twenty five feet above the ground and so settled into a comfortable position for the night. Sleep came easily to her exhausted body despite the cold and drizzly weather. Her dreams turned to nightmares. She felt she was caught up in a maelstrom between the sky and the earth below. Her body was being tossed around like a rag doll while her limbs seemed to become grotesquely disjointed.

Gabby awoke with a start, not sure at first where she was. She heard whispering from below and suddenly it all came back to her. She glanced down from her perch expecting to see her pursuers directly beneath the grand old oak. What she did see startled her.

The two dark skinned men were dressed in black and cradling shotguns as they walked toward the tree approximately a hundred yards away. Gabby sat back up and pondered how she could hear them so clearly from such distance. She leaned forward stretching. Her body ached all over especially her back, hands and feet. Looking at her legs she noticed no cuts or scratches from the night before.

'Very strange indeed,' she muttered to herself.

She listened intently to the approaching men. She knew they were speaking a harsh mixture of Romany/Armenian, the language of her dead father, because she'd been taught to recognise it from a young age. The words she didn't completely understand but the fact that strangers in Connemara were speaking it, was enough to make her worry.

Her eyes scanned the fields and hills for any potential rescuers but there was nobody to be seen. She thought she saw movement on the road a mile or so away but it was too far . . .

'Mother of God!!' she exclaimed softly, upon realizing that if she focused intently she could suddenly zoom in on the police car so far in the distance. So now that she had amazing hearing and sight, she wondered what other powers she had.

Leaning back into the trunk she looked down at her arms and legs. There was a caterpillar moving over her leg and so she cupped it up in her hands. Bringing it closer to her mouth she warned,

'Be careful little one. There could be shooting.'

She opened her hands and to her astonishment the caterpillar had become a fully fledged butterfly with the most incredible wing colours she'd ever seen. The creature flew around her head a couple of times before alighting on a branch below her on the hidden side from the men approaching the tree.

Gabby studied the wings beating hypnotically beneath. She needed to touch the velvety softness once more. So she slowly reached down for it with her left hand while grasping the trunk of the grand tree with her right. Inch by inch and totally mesmerized by the insect's beauty, she leaned over until her right fingers started to lose purchase on the damp bark and began to slip.

'Whoa!' she exclaimed as she tried to dig her nails into

the moist bark but to no avail. Just as she was past the point of no return, an amazing thing happened. Long silvery talons sprouted from her fingers and plunged easily into the oak tree halting her fall. She pulled herself upright catching a glimpse of the men running toward the tree, guns raised, searching the canopy for the source of the cry they'd just heard.

Gabby stood and squeezed herself tight to the trunk hoping to be invisible to their line of sight. She then took a moment to calm herself and examine the fingers of her right hand. There were no talons protruding. Nothing! They were as normal as they'd ever been. She was really scared now.

Did I dream it? Am I losing my mind?

The crack of a branch breaking below her bought her back to the danger she was in. The two men were now directly beneath her. It was only a matter of time before she was spotted. The tree was only partially foliaged now in late autumn and so she decided to try and climb higher to deeper cover. Of course, she reasoned, they might do the same but she knew she had the advantage of being much more agile than two grown men with heavy shotguns. Off in the distance Garda Mark Shanahan and Garda Sheila Russell were cruising slowly down a lane two miles west of last night's conflagration at the gypsy campsite. Jasper the bloodhound dozed on the back seat.

'Phew! Open the rear windows, will ya Sheila? What do ya feed that thing?'

Sheila Russell looked over in mock horror.

'*That thing?* Hope you're not referring to my baby.'

'As you well know, I am referring to your lazy lump of canine confusion prone on the backseat,' Mark said grinning

Sheila slid the rear windows down while trying hard to keep a straight face as the toxic cloud overwhelmed her.

'Jaysus dog!' she shrieked, stopping the car before jumping out the door.

Mark followed her immediately from the other side, the two of them bending over in hysterics. As the laughter waned they heard the distant sound of a gunshot. Jasper bolted upright, his bulbous nose protruding from the car window and ears pricked up.

'I'll call Special Weapons. You get the dog!' Shanahan screamed.

Russell wrapped the loose fitting lead around Jasper's head and let him out.

Meanwhile back at the tree one of the men had fired blindly up into the foliage to try to spook their quarry. It had worked.

Gabby panicked and climbed up the main trunk with reckless abandon. Twenty feet higher she stopped and listened. She could hear the metallic scrape of the firing pin ratcheting forward to ignite the cartridge. She moved to the far side, shielding herself with the trunk once more.

But she wasn't quick enough. The gun fired and she felt some of the pellets enter her foot. The pain was so intense that she screamed with such high pitch that neither she nor the men below could hear it. The only one who did was Jasper, the bloodhound, from a mile away. He pulled so hard on the leash that Garda Russell couldn't hold on and off he went bounding across the fields toward the giant oak.

Gabby was scared, incensed and shaking with rage at being shot. She turned her head searching the ground below when suddenly she caught a glimpse of something totally unreal. Her beautiful long wavy red hair was changing, from the ends up, to a brilliant white.

'What the . . ?' she exclaimed. As she stroked her now transformed hair, the long silver talons appeared once more from her fingers.

'This is definitely not normal.'

She moved her hands round and round examining the beauty of her new nails. She realized she no longer felt pain in her foot and when she looked down she could see no blood or any sign that she had been shot. As she continued to stare in amazement, silvery claws began to appear through her sandals. Without analyzing too much, she scaled up the tree trunk nearly to the top in seconds.

The two Romanies had managed to climb up to the lower branches. They scrutinized everything above but could see no sign of the girl. Just as they contemplated whether to continue upwards or not, they heard the howling of a bloodhound off in the distance, but moving closer.

They scuttled back down the tree, knowing if they were caught they would be put in jail for life. One man thought he could safely jump the last ten feet but he landed badly and sprained his ankle. Gabby craned her head until she could see what they were arguing over from her perch on high. One man was pleading with the other to help carry him but the first man would have none of it. He raised his gun and was about to shoot his accomplice at point blank range.

Gabby tried to conceal a squeal but couldn't, considering everything else that had already happened. The man raised his gun high into the tree and let off a barrage of shots before grabbing his partner under the arm and hobbling toward the river. Gabby was shaken but unhurt.

CHAPTER 4

Back at the patrol car, the Special Weapons Officer had arrived and was squinting through his telescopic sight at the gigantic tree in the distance. He'd never been a member of any police force anywhere. In fact many law agencies, including Interpol and the FBI, had been after him for years. His name was Willie Stix and he'd been in charge of the attack at the campsite the previous evening. Born in Germany, his real name was Willem Steigal and he was actually a master tactician. Last night he had screwed up. His patience was running thin at this stage. It had been easy for him to monitor the police radio band and end up at this location.

He became frustrated at the scenario playing out before his eyes. It seemed to him that two of his men had somehow attracted the attention of the local police. He needed to amend the situation. The Garda called Shanahan pointed out the direction in which his partner had run after the dog before chasing her himself.

Willie Stix could clearly see a man shooting up into the tree for some reason, yet unknown. He scanned up and down but couldn't make out anything, until he caught a reflection from near the top. It was an intense flash of light but the more he tried to make out the source, the more he thought his eyes must have been playing tricks on him.

Gabby saw that the dog was only a field away so she decided to stay flat against the trunk. Her grandfather had always told her to trust no one and so even the sight of the Garda following close behind was of little comfort.

Back on the ridge, Stix screwed the sight onto the huge Berretta .560 calibre sniping rifle he'd just retrieved from the boot of his car. It certainly wasn't the weapon most modern day snipers would use. It was cumbersome and heavy, but for this kind of distance it should prove very effective.

Garda Russell and Shanahan were closing in on Jasper, the barking less ferocious, the pace noticeably slower.

'Finally,' Russell exclaimed turning to her puffing partner.

'I never thought he'd stop,' she said, bending over with hands on knees.

'Whew! Not bad for a twelve year old. Are you armed?' she asked her partner.

Gardaí in Ireland generally are not, but since serious crime had increased over the last decade, some patrol cars had hidden compartments in the boot of their cars, in case of emergency. The first gunshot was enough for Shanahan to grab the small .25 millimetre Beretta and hide it inside his heavy corduroy jacket.

'Yep' he said patting his jacket.

Gabby watched in horror as the uninjured man below, knelt down behind a fallen branch and began taking aim at the two unaware Gardaí. She knew if she shouted a warning she would be as good as dead. Her mind was in turmoil with everything else that had gone on in the last twelve hours and now this. What could she do?

Willie Stix had no time to erect the tripod and so he leaned the long gun on the roof of the car. He was probably one of the best snipers anywhere in the world but this shot was going to be tricky. He watched as the two officers neared the huge oak tree. He then focused on the lead Garda. The man had pulled a handgun out of his jacket and was moving cautiously. The crosshair of his scope lined up with the back of Garda Shanahan's head.

Gabby, still high in the tree had only one option she could risk. She screamed that same high pitched screech she had done minutes before. Jasper freaked out and started howling at the tree. The two Gardaí hit the ground for safety reasons, not sure what was happening, leaving Stix a clear field of fire. He'd never had any qualms about shooting people, but in this instance he didn't need any more messes to clean up. His first shot struck the log behind which the men were hiding. It was intentional. He wanted them to disappear.

Gabby heard the shot exiting the barrel a mile away before anyone else. Her hearing was so attuned that it was actually as quick as the speed of sound. As the Romany stood to see where the bullet had come from, a long volley of shots peppered the log in front of him, causing the two of them to crawl away through the tall grass.

'This is Weapons here. You alright?' came a voice over the police radio.

'Fine . . . fine. That was you?' stuttered Shanahan. '

Aye, be down in a few. Secure the area, please,' was the reply.

'Er, yes sir. You want us to er give chase?' 'No need, I'll take care of it.'

A bewildered Russell looked at a more bewildered Shanahan.

'That was some shooting,' she said

'Unbelievable!' was all he could reply. 'That guy's good.'

Back at his car, after calling the two officers from theirs, Stix continued to search for the girl through his scope but to no avail. He could take them out but decided that would bring him too much attention. Besides, the police might have figured out what was going on by now.

He placed the gun back in the car and drove off down the road, listening intently for any chatter on the scanner that might lead him to his ultimate goal, killing the girl. Fifty thousand euro had been the price and since his foreign legion days he'd yet to fail an assignment.

CHAPTER 5

One hour later, after numerous conversations on the radio, Shanahan threw it on the ground in frustration.

'You're not going to believe this! According to *them*, there are no Special Weapons officers within fifty miles, and they never even received a request for back up.

Sheila stood, her hands on her hips.

'Huh, that's interesting, so what do we do now?' she gesticulated around the crime scene. 'We've done all the securing we can, so I suppose we head back up.'

'Great. I'm going over there to find Jasper.' Shanahan continued, 'Perhaps he knows who the shooter was!'

One hour later they gave up their search for the missing dog and walked back up the hill to their car.

Gabby had secured a relatively comfortable space in the tree. She'd been in tighter jams in her short life. The only thing she was concerned about was getting back down eventually. The talons had retracted as soon as she'd stopped climbing. She really hoped they'd appear once more on her descent. Otherwise, she supposed they might find her bones wrapped around the tree when it fell in another hundred years or so.

From her vantage point, she could see the guards reaching the road but still she dared not move a muscle.

'Tricky people these humans,' she said out loud before realizing that she was one of them.

'What a strange thing to say, bit like talking to yourself huh?' she giggled, not really sure if she was going a bit loopy. She started to feel a little ashamed for making light of the situation but then remembered her grandfather Gappy's quote When times are bad and you're feeling low, 'tis the time to smile, the time to glow. A tear ran down her cheek with the memory.

An hour later she decided to move. The fact that the gentle breeze was starting to blow harder made the decision easier. She concentrated all her thoughts on her descent from her brain down her arms and legs to her fingers and toes. Then, as hoped, her long silvery nails appeared.

It took her seconds to reach the branch she'd dozed upon when originally climbing the tree the previous night. Searching the fields and hedgerows with her eyes she spotted nothing threatening and so dropped to the soft damp grass below. Gabby stayed crouched low as she surveyed the area 360 degrees around the tree. She'd nearly finished the circle when suddenly she spotted a movement. A large head popped up in the long grass. Big bloodshot saucer-shaped eyes looked her over before moving forward.

Gabby stood transfixed as the bloodhound sauntered up to her. She recognized it and immediately thought the police were coming back, but she saw no sign. She reached out her hand to stroke it and got a slobbery tongue instead. Jasper came closer and promptly fell to the ground lying on his back expecting and receiving a tummy rub. Gabby noticed a piece of paper hooked under the collar. She scanned the area once more before opening it and reading 'Derryinver will be safer.' She turned the paper over trying to find any clues as to the identity of the sender but there were none. 'Huh?' she uttered in puzzlement, folding the note and putting it in her pocket. Either way, she decided, it must be a trap. The police or the shooter but which could it be? It could be whoever sent it was trying a little reverse psychology or not.

The small fishing village of Derryinver was closer but this time of year not very busy and so she reasoned there would be more eyes idling and ogling from behind lace curtains overlooking the pier than in Cleggan.

Cleggan had more ferries constantly servicing the islands out in the Atlantic and so people would be less curious and more intent on the loading and unloading of provisions than paying attention to her. She decided on Cleggan and to keep a weary eye open at all times for anyone paying her more than a passing interest. Off she set, heading for the forest that led to the 'Bog Road' to Cleggan. By her reckoning she could be there by nightfall. Gabby turned and pointed at the dog pretty sure in her knowledge that he would not obey.

'Stay! Lie Down! No!' She turned to walk once more and heard the unmistakable panting and drooling behind her. Kneeling down she held his big head in her hands and searched his eyes for any malevolent tendencies. She felt nothing malicious in the old dog, only good intent. She stood up and pondered for a second.

'Jack!' 'That's it. I'll call you Jack.'

Gabby walked off once more this time with her new friend by her side. Although the journey was dangerous, it wasn't her main concern. It was getting chilly and her night clothes were ripped and torn. She remembered there was a loggers' hut deep in the forest from the days she and her brothers would go there to steal firewood. Maybe she could find something useful to wear. And so, on they went crossing the fields and boglands of Western Ireland, staying away from any isolated cottages or farms for fear of meeting anyone.

It was nearly dusk when they reached the forest and, as they entered, it suddenly became more like night amongst the towering evergreens. It seemed to Gabby that her earlier memories of life were returning to her easily and with more frequency. She deduced it must be because of the transitions of mind and body, her mother had told her would come on turning sixteen. They reached the log shed without detour and saw a thick padlock securing the door. She sized up her fingers and soon dismissed the idea of extending her talons for a more practical approach. Jack sniffed the area and came back to her showing no cause for alarm. She picked up a small rock, felt its weight and decided it would do the job.

On her first attempt the rock slipped off the lock and, as a result ,she painfully skinned her knuckles.

'Oh crap!!' she screamed in frustration sucking away the blood.

'Good thing' she said to Jack, giggling, 'that I didn't have my claws out. Might have stabbed myself' Jack agreed with a cautionary yelp. The second time was better and she hit the rusting padlock full on. It nearly gave. The third time worked like a charm and the lock fell to the ground in pieces.

Inside there were boxes to sit on and a table of sorts made from a large outside edge cut of a once fine tree. On the table was a paraffin lantern still half full with the purple liquid. A big box of matches lay alongside old grimy plates and scattered knives and forks.

Once the light was lit, she opened some of the boxes and found,much to her excitement, relatively clean blankets and a couple of thick winter coats.

'Look Jack, we'll be warm for the night.' she said excitedly, feeling a bit like a kid again, she thought to herself knowing those days of innocence were now well passed.

The night, like the previous one, brought even stranger nightmares. There was a girl similar to her wearing grey or black robes, face contorted unnaturally, spinning like a whirling dervish or human tornado, slicing through bodies with ease while a dog similar to Jack, lay on the ground yelping in pain. The dream became so disturbing it actually woke her up.

Or maybe it wasn't the dream; maybe something else had disturbed her sleep. She crept forward from under the blanket, gently touching Jack as she passed, 'Sssh,' she whispered. To her surprise he seemed to understand.

She reached the door and heard low talking coming from somewhere not too distant from the hut. She cursed herself for not at least putting the broken lock back on the hasp, so a casual look might have given them a little more time. She cracked the door and peered out into the gloom of rising dawn. Moving cautiously up the lumber track were two men dressed in black and carrying guns like the other two the day before. She knew that seeing two didn't mean there weren't more in the trees and so she made a decision. Finding an old piece of rope she slipped it through Jack's collar and led him up to the door. 'Ready old boy?' she questioned inching the door open further and silently crawling toward the closest trees pulling the aged bloodhound behind her.

Jack seemed quite unaware of what was happening until, within a couple of feet of being safe in the forest, he caught a whiff of the hunters. He strained against the lead and it snapped sending him bounding and howling off down the track. Gabby knew she couldn't risk exposure and so slipped behind a large fir. She watched in horror as the two men, no longer caught by surprise, began to raise their weapons.

Before they could shoot, she heard an altogether different noise coming from the rear of the hut. It was the sound of metal scraping on metal and then fibre of some kind being pulled taut. She had little time to ponder what it was before she caught the flash of an arrow being released and entering the soft fur of her new found friend, Jack. It stopped his momentum completely and he fell in a heap to the ground in front of the two men.

As the crossbowman ran forward with cheers at his

brilliance, and the other two stood relieved, Gabby released a bone-shaking scream that sent birds flying into the air for miles around.

The three men, now grouped together, turned in unison, staring in horror, at what they saw next. Gabby lost all sense of caution, or even reality, as she charged the hunters, screaming hysterically and waving her arms. Her talons fully extended, her hair turning completely white, her face seemed to elongate becoming slightly more aerodynamic.

Only the man with the crossbow had time to react. He quickly strung an arrow aimed and fired. Gabby caught it in mid flight spun and launched it back at him with ten times the force it had left the bow. It entered his chest briefly before exiting his back and sticking in the arm of one of the men behind.

Gabby stopped a few yards away as if to challenge them to take a shot, but they would have none of it. They turned and ran down the hill faster than they'd probably ever run before.

She knelt down beside Jack stroking his head and whispering comforting words in his ear. By the time she'd calmed herself, her body had reverted back to normality.

The arrow had hit the old bloodhound in the hind quarters making walking impossible. Gabby picked him up as gently as she could and walked quickly into the forest.

CHAPTER 6

An hour later she could see the islands of Inishbofin and Inishturk off in the distance. This meant Cleggan village was only four or five miles below the rolling hills of bogland in this isolated part of the world.

They stopped on the edge of the forest, Gabby checking for any movement, other than sheep. She lay Jack down on a clump of lavender-coloured heather that grows wild everywhere in this moist peaty soil. She knew she had to do something now, because there was no way he'd last until she found a vet; something she didn't want to do in any case.

Jack's big droopy eyes looked up at her. He was calm and still, almost as if he knew the end was near.

'Stay alive Jack,' she said. 'This will hurt. Be brave.'

Once more she scanned the trees for any signs of strangers. When she was sure they were safe, she concentrated on releasing the talons of the thumb and index finger of her right hand. Once this was accomplished, she rubbed them together fast causing much friction and heat, thus sterilizing them.

First, she moved to where the arrow had entered his skin and with a sharp pincer movement she cut the shaft.

She threw it away in disgust. Then, heating her nails once more, she plunged her index finger into the wound and, carefully lifting his body with her left arm, pushed the tip out the other side. Jack gave a half-hearted yelp before slipping once more into unconsciousness. She turned and wiped her hands on some grass and then peered down to see if the hole was any worse.

Amazingly, there was no longer any hole to see. The wound had cauterized itself with the heat of the talon.

'Wow! Cool!' she exclaimed.

She removed the jacket she'd stolen from the hut and wrapped it around Jack. He was breathing gently and so she moved away a few feet and squatted down on a hillock surveying the land wondering what else could possibly happen. She let her mind go into a trancelike state, almost like the total linking of body and soul as one, for the first time in her life. She saw swatches of yellows and greens, reds and blues signifying to her the beauty all around and then the blacks and greys of death and destruction.

Minutes, or maybe hours, later, she suddenly felt a presence behind her. She turned slowly, fully alert. What she saw made her laugh with happiness. Standing there was Jack, head high, tongue drooling and tail wagging furiously. She leapt down and gave him the biggest hug, like a long lost friend who had returned.

'C'mon Jack, let's get the show on the road,' she said following a sheep trail down the hills toward Cleggan.

Two hours later they stopped behind a ruined stone cottage, prevalent in these parts from the days of The Great Famine, when millions of Irish died or emigrated to America. They sniffed the air. It smelled of rain coming. Looking far out to sea Gabby saw the rolling black clouds common for Eastern Atlantic storms this time of year. She shivered involuntarily and pulled the jacket around her. Sure enough, within ten minutes the heavens opened and the wind blew stronger and stronger. As they crouched behind an old stone wall, she could smell the food being prepared by Mary, the cook, in Oliver's pub. It made her realise she hadn't eaten in at least twenty four hours.

'Well, that's something we must remedy. What do you think Jack, you hungry?' she said out loud. Jack growled instead of giving his customary bark which surprised her until she realised it could have been a warning instead.

Too late. She focused her olfactory senses, immediately picking up the smell of French tobacco. Gitanes or Gauloises, if she recalled correctly. That was another thing she'd been taught to recognise from childhood.

Before she could react, the figure of a man stepped out in front of her. In the dim light she saw he was a small stocky man wearing a bright yellow slicker and Greek fisherman's cap. He looked, to Gabby, about as unthreatening as anyone she'd ever met. But looks can be deceiving. Jack snapped and snarled at the stranger and Gabby grabbed his collar before any damage was done.

She looked at the man once more, focusing in on his face. He was very calm and untroubled. He had a peaceful presence about him, slightly tanned, large nose, blue eyes under round rain-soaked spectacles. She thought he looked a bit like that Indian guy. What was his name? Ghandi. That was it.

'Allo Mademoiselle, ca va?' the Frenchman asked.

Gabby had picked up a limited amount of French in school. 'Oui,' was all she could think to reply.

'Can I help you?' she asked rather forcefully.

The Frenchman gave an exaggerated bow whilst removing his cap. He was completely bald lending more credence to Gabby's first thoughts.

'Mais non, Mademoiselle. It is I who can help you,' he said with a toothless grin. He knelt down putting out his hand.

'Please, let your dog go and we'll soon see if I am to be trusted.'

She didn't hesitate. Releasing Jack, he rushed forward

snarling and barking but stopped at the outstretched hand. He sniffed it a couple of times, turned around and trotted back to Gabby. She felt a great deal of relief at this.

'Nice to meet someone not trying to kill me,' she said light-heartedly, as if a load had been lifted off her young shoulders.

'Let's go somewhere a bit drier, non?'

Gabby nodded. They walked through some fields, over a stile, reaching a recently completed holiday cottage overlooking Cleggan village.

'Attend, you wait here. I will go through the back and let you in the front.'

Gabby and Jack were tired and wet and so they sat on the stoop until a minute later the door opened, so in they went.

'Sit down, s'il vous plaît. I go get some towels for you.'

Gabby sat on the dust-covered couch. Jack lay at her feet.

'Do you have any food? We're starving.'

He handed her a couple of beach towels and headed into the kitchen. She heard cabinets being opened and closed. He reappeared holding a can of soup and one of beans.

'Which one you like?'

Gabby looked down at Jack.

'He'll have the beans, I'll have the soup, please.'

The Frenchman gave the thumbs up and returned to the kitchen.

Gabby stood and walked around the living room. There were pictures of a young family, though none of her host she observed. She ambled down the corridor, looking for a bathroom. She found one near the back door. She noticed broken glass on the tiles obviously from the small square pane that was missing enabling an intruder to gain access to the home.

The Frenchman leaned over the stove, humming softly to himself, stirring the food with his back to the hall.

Gabby stealthily moved to the edge of the table, hoisted herself up onto it, barely causing even a ripple in the air. She focused on the back of his head as if trying to read his thoughts. He was so intent on his work he didn't hear anything until she said,

'Who are you and why did you break in?'

He turned so suddenly that he knocked one of the saucepans onto the floor, exclaiming,

'Mon Dieu!! You scare me! I break in because we need somewhere to shelter. Mac tell me you unusual girl but not you move like a ghost.'

'You know, knew, my grandfather?' she asked warily.

'Oh yes, as I know your name Gabriella. Has something happened to him?' he asked.

'He's dead! They're all dead, at the campsite last night. We were attacked.' she said, voice cracking. He softly laid his hand on her shoulder.

'The Romanies do this?'

'I presume so, I just don't understand why,' she sobbed. He helped her off the table and into a chair, shaking his head.

'Come, little one, we eat first and then we talk.'

Jack wandered over and ate the spilt beans off the floor. Once all were sated he cleared his throat.

'My name is Philippe Dumas. I met your grandfather a long, long time ago at The Festival of Gypsies which is held every year in the south of France. This you might know?'

'I've heard of it but was never allowed to go. Too dangerous, everyone said.'

'Well, for you it would be. It was where your mother and father met. You know the story, right?'

'Met? He forced himself on her and I am the result.' The words came spitting from her mouth. 'I presume this you didn't know?' He looked stunned as he contemplated this news.

'So this blood feud against you and your family is

because . . . ?'

'Because- this is just rumour over the years- my grandfather murdered my father and his brother when he heard news of the'- she hesitated-' . . . deed.'

'So, the other part of the story, the bit your grandfather told me, the real reason they are after you?'

Gabby looked puzzled. 'I don't understand, what other part are you talking about?'

Philippe leaned forward and took her hand, 'Cherie, he told me that because your father was the son of the seventh son of the seventh son that if his first child is a girl she will bring terrible destruction and tragedy upon his clan. This is why they seek you out.'

Philippe released her hand as she stood. She watched Jack finish the beans. She was about to say something when she heard a faint scuffling noise from the back door. She put her finger to her lips.

In a split second, Gabby caught sight of movement outside the kitchen window. It was a blur to her but she knew immediately it was the blur of a human face. She signalled to Philippe to make no sound or movement. She concentrated hard for several seconds, using her newly acquired senses.

'No, Philippe. It's okay. I feel no threat here.'

'Can I come in?' came a woman's voice from outside.

'Yes, you can as long as you've no gun' replied Gabby.

They stood on each side of the door as it creaked open. Jack was the first to react by emitting a low growl. The female police officer looked puzzled as her pet continued to growl softly. She knelt down saying,

'What's wrong boy? Remember me?' J

Jack sidled forward cautiously and allowed her to pet the top of his head. Garda, Sheila Russell, stood scrutinizing the Frenchman first and then, her face softening, Gabby.

'You must be the girl that escaped from the campsite, am I right?' she asked with what seemed like genuine concern.

Gabby pointed to a chair, then turning to Philippe she said, 'Any tea?' Philippe nodded as Sheila sat, Gabby taking the seat opposite.

'What do you want?' Gabby asked harshly, 'Are you really a garda?' 'Why are you following me?' Did you write the note?' 'Why? Why? Why?'

She put her head in her hands, overwhelmed by everything going on, who to trust and should she trust anyone at all. Sheila laid her hand on Gabby's to try and comfort her but that didn't work too well.

As Gabby slowly raised her head her talons extended as her hair turned white. Sheila tried to stay calm as the girl held her hand, nails like silver knives.

Philippe walked in with the tea, saw what was happening and said,

'Gabriella, stop!'

Lowering the cups to the table, Gabby released the hand, retracting the claws once more. She picked up the tea, blew on it and took a sip.

'Hot, thank you.'

Sheila was shocked by what she'd just witnessed.

'That was amazing, scary, but still amazing.'

Gabby sipped her tea, analyzing Sheila through the rising steam.

'So the rumours are true' added Sheila.

'Suppose they are. What exactly has it to do with you?' Gabby asked, irritated once more.

'Your mother, Caitlan, and I went to school together, up till a few days before you were born when she had to leave, naturally. I wouldn't say we were close friends, but I was more willing to accept her as a girl rather than a traveller.'

'So what? All I'm hearing are words, words, words.'

'So, she told me about your conception with a Romany called Menjanii and his subsequent death at the hands of your grandfather.'

'Yes?' Gabby was losing patience

'Well, in the last year your mother contacted me many times, keeping me updated on the situation and asked me to watch for you if ever the need arose. So, here I am.'

'And I should believe you why exactly?'

Sheila looked hurt and slightly taken aback.

'Funny my mother never mentioned you to me considering we talked for hours just about every day,' Gabby said, yawning.

Gabby sipped her tea, glancing occasionally over to Philippe who was rubbing Jack's tummy on the floor. He seemed nervous.

'What's the name of your dog?' she asked

'Jasper.'

The dog lifted his head but couldn't make the transition from tummy rub to owner obedience.

'So, you sent the note and followed, GPS of some kind in the collar I presume?' Sheila nodded.

'Is Cleggan safe, or are there more killers outside just waiting for the signal?'

Philippe shrugged. Before either answered she said,

'Before you answer I need you both to write down the word.

Gabby caught the quick look of puzzlement between the two, her senses tried to warn her but she was too tired to think rationally.

The word'? What word are you talking about Gabriella?' Philippe asked.

Before she could answer she felt a stinging pain in her neck. As she started blacking out she managed to slash back and felt her talons connect with flesh. Philippe moved forward slowly as she crumpled to the floor.

Sheila dropped the syringe on the floor, checked that the gash on her arm wasn't deep and spat out the words,

'Forget the gun, give me the manacles and hurry. I don't know how long she'll be unconscious.'

Philippe produced two sets of cast iron handcuffs from

his backpack and another syringe. After they had secured her hands and feet, Sheila used some duct tape around the cut on her arm, Philippe asked,

'What did she mean by *write the word?*'

Sheila sat down wiping her brow with her sleeve.

'A code word I presume, or just a ploy. She's a quick thinker this one.'

Philippe nodded, 'You have the van outside?'

'Yes, we must hurry. Let's roll her up in the rug just in case there's anyone watching.'

She started pulling Gabby's legs over the edge of the carpet while Philippe lifted her head. Gabby's eyes shot open as her hair transformed to brilliant white. With talons extended she let out a glass-shattering shriek. Both Philippe and Sheila covered their ears. Jack howled incessantly.

Sheila signed to the Frenchman for the other syringe and plunged it into the girl's neck. Gabby blacked out once more.

They lifted Gabby into the back of the van, tightly securing her to lengths of steel chains especially welded into the truck frame on either side. They slammed the doors, locking them by sliding the heavy bolt across the outside. Once the padlock was closed, the van became a steel box with no windows or side doors.

'How much serum did you give her?' Philippe asked, concern in his voice.

'Enough to kill a horse, but I don't know how long it's going to last. I'll check on her later,' Sheila said going back inside the house.

'What about the dog?' he asked.

'Shoot him, I have no attachment there He'd only get in the way.'

Philippe didn't like to kill animals so he aimed left and the shot sent Jack off running.

Willie Stix had been following Sheila from a distance.

He was sure he'd met her once before prior to the oak tree incident. Through his infra red telescopic sight he'd more or less witnessed everything that had occurred in the cottage. She and the little guy seemed to have control of the situation and so when he saw the carpet being carried out into the van he decided to follow anyway, just in case. He couldn't afford another screw up.

Philippe went into the house grinning with anticipation of the night with Sheila.

CHAPTER 7

The motion of the van on the bumpy roads of Ireland caused Gabby to stir many hours later. Her eyes couldn't penetrate the darkness but her other senses could. Touch, smell and hearing told her in what she was being held.

Up in the front seats the adrenaline was pumping fast.

'We did it!' screamed Sheila, perspiration running down her face.

'A 100,000 euro, 50,000 for each for us, incroyable! We are bad, non?' said Phillipe leaning over and kissing his partner in crime. The twosome had done many jobs together over the years, but none as financially fruitful as this one.

Gabby's situation reminded her of a movie she'd seen once where the person was tied to the rack and stretched until their body was pulled apart. She knew nobody was pulling her apart but her chains were tightly secured to each side of the van and so any movement was severely limited.

'I am so stupid!' she screamed, wriggling her body this way and that, but to no avail. These people were well–prepared, she thought to herself. She knew if she remained in this van it would end badly. She extended her talons and tried to saw through a link in the chain, soon realising she was getting nowhere fast. In frustration she arched her back pulling hard with both feet and hands. The harder she pulled the more her vertebrae separated causing her nerves and tendons to stretch apart.

Gabby had pulled and strained against the chains holding her, the final stage of her metamorphosis had begun. She had manoeuvred herself until she was nearly doubled over, stretching each of the metal links a few millimeters apart. Her talons screeched in an effort to give her a little more purchase on the metal floor. Suddenly, the pain in her back and between her shoulders became so intense, she let out a scream of such magnitude that, unbeknown to her, she'd shattered the windows in the van and the car being driven by Willie Stix, half a mile behind.

The skin parted from the base of her skull to her lower back. There was no blood. She lay flat on the floor as her folded wings unfurled themselves for the first time in sixteen years. They each spanned six feet in length, easily touching the roof of the van.

She felt tiny pin pricks all over her body as millions of brilliant white feathers pushed out through her skin. Moving her left wing, she laid it down beside her on the floor. Then, with much effort, she shuffled her body until she was on her side next to the wing, leaving her right wing free to move around an enclosed space such as this.

With little concern, and even less effort, she pushed the wing tip into the ceiling of the van, cutting through it easier than a knife would through butter. In the gloomy light she could now see how they had tied her down. She brought her wing down to the manacles by bending it without difficulty.

Once free of her bonds she jumped out through the hole in the roof and upon hearing Philippe and Sheila cocking their guns, she leapt skyward, her new and powerful wings beating strongly. She hovered a thousand feet up. With her greatly improved eyesight she could see for miles.

Philippe and Sheila were laughing and planning what they were going to spend the money on when suddenly all the van windows blew out. Sheila slammed on the brakes. They looked at each other, fear and uncertainty growing in their eyes. Without a word, they popped in the clips on their Sig Sauers, checking how many rounds between them. They nodded in unison and exited the van.

They examined the outside of the van together rather than split up and do a side each. They knew the kid had powers beyond the ordinary and the thought of one of those razor sharp talons lopping off an appendage or two made them decide to stick together.

Philippe listened intently, placing his ear on the cold metal.

'Rien,' he whispered to Sheila.

At the rear doors the padlock was still intact.

'You open it. I'll cover you,' he said standing back and pointing his gun.

'Don't shoot me,' Sheila said as she slid the bolt back and threw open the doors.

The van was empty, the roof peeled back like a tin can. No sign of the girl. The little Frenchman jumped up into the van and examined the roof and chains. He stupidly touched one of the manacles and received a serious burn.

'Merde!' he exclaimed before putting his fingers into his mouth to help cool them. After a minute he scrutinised the roof once more.

'It's like it's melted as if it has been cut with something,' he said looking toward Sheila at the door. She looked very scared now turning her head quickly in all directions before focusing on Philippe once more.

'Let's get out of here . . . now, before it's too . . . What?' She saw the change in his eyes before she could finish the sentence. He was focusing on something behind her. She turned slowly.

Sheila followed his gaze, shielding her eyes from the

rising of the sun. All she saw were a couple of birds in the sky and distant hills and trees.

'What is it?' she asked.

Philippe pointed to what looked like a large bird, maybe an albatross or seagull, she thought to herself but the more she stared the more she realized it was flying much too fast for any kind of avian species she'd ever encountered.

Without hesitation, Gabby manoeuvred the giant wings in every direction, learning quickly the incredible mobility she now possessed. She was mesmerized by the razor-like edge and thousands of intermeshed white feathers on each wing. Although her wavy hair was still red, the more she looked down at the couple beside the van the more incensed she became, resulting in her hair changing to white once more.

She felt ready to test her new potential and so, without hesitation, she folded her wings to her side, propelling her body earthward at a staggering speed. Philippe and Sheila braced against each other in terror at the sight of the apparition coming toward them. Gabby's wings fully opened fifty feet away as she landed gracefully upright letting them fall to her side. She still wore her shorts but the T-shirt had long ago fallen into tatters. As she got closer, Philippe could see that her whole body was covered by tiny white feathers, protecting her nudity. She stopped twenty feet away.

Raising her right hand Gabby said,

'Please put down the guns, I'll not hurt you.'

Sheila and Philippe looked hard at each other. He started to lower his but Sheila kept hers aimed at the girl.

'Hurt us? Ha ha. You'll not hurt us!' Her finger moved against the trigger.

'Stop it! She'll kill us if you shoot!' Philippe screamed but to no avail.

'Kill us? Not if she's dead she won't!'

Gabby heard the spring in the gun's trigger being stretched taut just before it fired. She released her talons in the raised hand and caught the bullet between thumb and index finger. Philippe dropped his weapon in awe but Sheila after only a second's hesitation fired again and again emptying the clip. Just as the second bullet was fired Gabby pulled her left wing around shielding her body from the onslaught. Some of the rounds pinged off the wing's almost metal-like leading edge, some just stuck in the meshed wing feathers. None affected Gabby physically in any way. Mentally, however, she was a seriously angry girl.

As Sheila fumbled to reload Philippe dropped his gun in horror at what he was witnessing. Gabby's eyes glowed red, her hair was white, her face contorted, as she launched herself toward her adversary. Although her wings were separate appendages from her arms, in this instance, she hooked her hands into the pouches at the end of each wing, giving herself extra forward thrust.

Sheila knew she was too late. The movement of air against her face told her so. She let the clip drop as she looked up. Gabby's wings were spread wide. Her pupils were now deep yellow, the 'whites of her eyes' blood red. Keeping her wings fully raised she disconnected her arms and held them out for the guns.

Both Sheila and Philippe placed the guns in each hand. With arms perfectly still Gabby's talons extended themselves from each finger and with lightening speed shredded the metal to pieces. After letting the bits fall to the ground she crossed her arms over her chest, keeping her wings outstretched.

Philippe feigned having a heart attack in order to distract the girl, grasping at his chest, leaving his partner one last chance to gain the upper hand. As Gabriella turned toward the commotion Sheila slid a long hunting knife from the sheath concealed behind her back. Before

Gabby could react the knife was thrust into her chest below her rib cage. The pain was intense as she dropped her right hand, slashing right through Sheila's wrist, leaving her hand almost comically alone clutching the knife on the ground. Sheila grabbed the stump of her arm with her other hand and fell to her knees.

Gabby stared hard at the Frenchman before striking him with her right wing tip flat side out knocking him to the ground, unconscious. Then, with her left hand she plucked out the knife and with her right she grasped Sheila around the neck, pulling her to her feet and then off the ground, closer to her now smoldering eyes. Sheila tried to close hers but was unable to as Gabby released a high pitched screech creating instantaneous pain throughout her body. Gabby's eyes rolled up in their sockets causing beams of molten light to shoot into Sheila's. Her irises were temporarily burned in that brief few seconds. She dropped her to the ground, leaving her partially blind and deaf.

Gabby stood statuesque for several minutes before the pain in her side brought her back to reality. The pain wasn't as intense as before and so using the same method as with Jack, the day before, she cauterized the wound with heated talons.

As Sheila wailed and stumbled blindly down the road, Gabby retracted both wings and talons. She was just a teenager once more. She walked around to the cab of the van and pulled out a waterproof jacket that had belonged to the Garda. She put it on and zipped it up. She walked over to Philippe and sized up his pants. Unembarrassed by the male form -she had grown up with four brothers after all- she removed them and tried them on. They were a bit too short but they'd do.

Philippe began to come to, sitting up, focusing his eyes and rubbing his sore head. It was then he noticed Gabby, arms by her side, standing in front of him wearing his trousers. He found it hard to comprehend that a girl, so innocent looking, could wreak such havoc on two armed adults.

'Get up.' Gabby ordered.

Philippe stood up shakily still rubbing his head.

'You know what I am capable of, so now I need some answers, okay?' Philippe nodded without enthusiasm.

'Were you and that woman over there,' Gabby asked pointing down the road, 'part of the original attack, or were you a backup plan?'

He stared off down the road as if noticing his beloved Sheila for the first time,

'What did you do to her?' he asked.

'I will do the same to you unless you answer my questions!' she screamed, trying to snap him back to reality.

He turned to her once more, his eyes darting around.

'We were hired in case you lived through the initial onslaught' he whispered.

'Who hired you?' she hissed.

'Don't know, never knew. Some guy called Willie was the middle man. Never told us anything, I swear to you,' he said, listlessly moving away from her and after his love.

Gabby let him go.

Willie Stix had continued to follow them. As soon as his windows blew in, he jammed on the brakes. He wasn't sure of the cause so he slid out of the car and crawled to the boot, removing his sniper rifle. Peering around the bumper he could see the Garda and her friend, guns drawn moving to the back of their van. He had no idea what had caused the windows to shatter so took the opportunity to crab-walk up a hillock nearby and find a good sniping angle. Lying on the hillock, he adjusted the sights once more and honed in on the van ahead.

Gabby brushed the bits of glass off the seats in the van

and started it up. Although she didn't have a licence, her grandpa had taught her to drive when she was ten. One of the few advantages of growing up a traveller was the knowledge of the roads and towns of Ireland. She was sure she was past Limerick and had been heading south, probably to Cork, from where ferry boats sailed regularly to France.

She turned off the ignition and surveyed the landscape around her. Everything had happened so quickly. She pondered her mother's words:

Be aware. Watch, look listen and you'll always be safe.

Gabby slipped out of her clothes and by the time her feet touched the ground her transition was complete. She needed to be sure no one had seen what had happened in the last few minutes.

She lifted off cautiously, spinning gently around in circles by merely moving one hand forward and the other back. Higher and higher she went, her ears and eyes fully attuned for anything untoward.

She focused on a car way back down the winding road with blown-out windows. She could see hundreds of tiny specks of broken glass on the dashboard

'Ooops' she said to herself. 'I wonder what happened to the owner?'

She turned and flew toward the car, her eyes focusing on the dashboard in case the driver's head popped up. Because of the reflective nature of the minute shards of glass she initially missed the flash off Willie Stix's telescopic sight.

Gabby saw the flash on the hill and heard the firing pin ignite the gunpowder in the cartridge. In an instinctive reaction she moved her right wing across to protect her face and body. In that millisecond, the bullet pinged off her wing's titanium edge and dropped harmlessly to the ground. Gabby wasted no time. She completely relaxed her mind and body letting herself spiral down out of control.

Stix watched in amazement as the girl collapsed in midair falling like a stone toward the earth. He knew he wanted to get a good look at what she was but decided on safety first. He ran for his car.

As Gabby neared the ground she spotted a man with a rifle running toward the road. She was really mad now. She'd also noted the hedge that ran alongside the field and so as soon as she was hidden from his view she opened her magnificent wings and flew directly at him, a mere two feet off the tarmac.

She was like a girl possessed, flying faster and faster toward the looming gate she was sure he would come through. The timing couldn't have been better. Just as Willie Stix reached the top of the gate Gabby appeared from behind the hedge. Not slowing down she plucked him from his perch causing his rifle to drop. She carried him high into the air, her talons digging into his muscled shoulders. Stix didn't even cry out. He knew he was in trouble.

After flying a couple of miles carrying such a weight Gabby began to tire. She descended into a deserted meadow and dropped him ten feet to the ground. She stayed above him circling, scrutinizing the man.

'Were you at the campsite?' she asked, finally landing in front of him letting her wings drop to her side.

He searched Gabby's eyes for any clue of her intentions before answering.

'Sure I was. I kill people,' he said, reaching for the gun hidden in the small of his back.

Just as he aimed, Gabby knelt down on one knee bringing her right wing around in an arc. The razor sharp titanium edged wing sliced neatly through the assassin's neck. She turned and took off so fast Willie Stix's head hadn't touched the ground by the time she was half way back to the van.

Slipping on her clothes once more, Gabby turned the van around to head back the way she'd come. She saw the other two assassins in the distance. Head bowed, Philippe cowered while holding onto Sheila. Neither made eye contact as she sped back toward Connemara.

Gabby had no regrets about the last hour. They had started it. She would finish it.

CHAPTER 8

It was lunchtime when Gabby reached Cleggan village. She left the van at the end of a dirt track occasionally used by hunters a couple of miles away. She had been squatting in the bushes for thirty minutes or so surveying the house where so many mistakes had been made. She needed to check for any kind of clue as to who wanted her dead so badly. She also wanted to see if Jack was okay.

The whole idea was crazy. What if they were waiting for her?

'Whatever will be, will be,' she muttered to herself.

She'd always been stubborn and somewhat indifferent to what others called commonsense. She knew if Philippe had called anyone else to tell of her escape she could be in trouble but she reasoned that he wouldn't want them to hear of his failure for fear of retribution against his and Sheila's families.

After another half an hour she approached the rear door with the shattered pane. Only it wasn't broken anymore. She looked around the ground for any telltale signs of broken glass and suddenly thought maybe she'd got the wrong house. Kneeling gently in the dirt she spotted one tiny fleck off to the side of the door stoop. Whoever had cleaned up had been meticulous, bordering on obsessive.

She walked to the side and pulled herself up by the window ledge to see if Jack was still there. The window tint was too strong even for her eyes. There was nothing else for it she decided. Looking at her fingers and then examining the lock, she chose the pinky finger on her right hand. Her smallest talon slid out as she slipped it into the door handle lock. Turning it delicately, the door opened. She moved inside quickly closing it behind her.

'Jack' she whispered as loudly as she dared, 'Jack, come here, it's okay.' There was nothing, no sound, no smell. She walked into the kitchen. The place was spotless. She scratched her head moving to the front window. Although it had been dark she knew this was the right house.

'Jack!' she said.

Nothing.

She searched cupboards and closets for any hint of the Frenchman but found no clue. She left the house quickly and quietly, closing the door behind her. Up on the hill she knelt in the damp grass knowing she shouldn't do what she was about to. Gabby cupped her hands up to her mouth and let out a long ear-popping wail. There was no barking in response and so she did it again, this time without the hands. She just let loose the highest pitch shriek as she could muster. That seemed to work, she thought to herself as every dog for miles started a chorus of baying and barking. She knew she'd have to change position quickly so crouching down she moved toward the west side of Cleggan.

A few minutes later she stopped, cocking her ear. She was sure she'd heard something unusual. Next thing you know, the howling got closer and closer as Jack came barreling out of the ferns knocking her flying into a muddy pool of brackish water while landing full weight on top of her. He licked and slobbered all over her until finally she managed to push him off, spluttering and spitting out the foul-tasting water.

She was laughing so hard her wet hands kept slipping off his head. Finally she hooked his collar.

'Keep still!' Jack, sit!' she cried out with laughter while trying to unhook the metal clasps securing it to his neck. She presumed the GPS was still inside it. It was the only explanation of how Sheila had tracked her.

It took several minutes of shrieking laughter and slobbery licks to find the small remote locator. She placed it in her pocket knowing that if she broke it they would become suspicious. If she threw it onto a truck they would think it strange, Jack not being a greyhound. They were clever people whoever they were, with several backup plans. Leaving Jack in the vicinity, should she return, was one of them. Sheila must have relayed Gabby's capture whilst she was unconscious in the van. If they were two steps ahead then she'd have to be four.

They made their way down toward the beach, the sun shining brightly after the deluge of rain the night before. She was well-used to the sudden changes in the weather in Ireland. Gabby stopped near a barn listening intently to the two farmers she'd spied from atop the hill. They seemed to be picking out cattle for the slaughterhouse. She knew the abattoir was located in Clifden, seven miles away and also that the speed of the tractor plus load would be very slow. She whispered to Jack to sit and stay knowing full well he probably wouldn't. Didn't matter if they were seen anyway, just a girl and her dog out walking. Erring on the side of caution, she tucked her hair in under the hood of her coat. If people asked questions later she wasn't going to make it any easier than it had to be. As she approached the tractor trailer the men looked up.

'Grand day now,' one said to her.

She nodded as if caught out and replied,

'Oui, er yes il fait beau, non?'

'Ah French are ya? Always liked the French.' The younger said with a grin.

As she came alongside the cart she pointed with her right hand toward the harbour, while hiding the GPS in her left.

'The ferry, er, c'est la, there?'

The two men glanced down to the port nodding in the affirmative as she dropped the device into the cattle cart. She hoped to herself that it wouldn't be stepped on too quickly.

'Er, thank you,' she said, waving to the men as she and Jack walked on down the hill.

Once at the bottom they turned back and walked along the rocky shore away from the village. There were several downturned currachs above the high tide mark but none looked seaworthy enough to travel five or six miles against the often cruel eastern Atlantic.

Gabby knew an outboard motor would be next to impossible to come by for two reasons. First, the theft of one would be reported much more quickly than just a missing anonymous boat. Secondly, she had no money to purchase one let alone buy the diesel to run it. She knew she had the strength to row that far as long as the weather stayed reasonable, another thing no betting person in these parts would wager on.

She sat down on the beach, exhausted and starving. After removing Philippe's pants she had also removed his T-shirt, so at least she was warm. Things weren't all bad she reasoned. She sat up, arms on knees, Jack passed out beside her. She knew she had to eat before attempting such a difficult row to a person she hardly knew in a place she'd never been or even seen.

The only knowledge she had was from her mother, who had said the island was shaped like a U with a huge stand of evergreens in the middle. She had also told her not to try to enter the little bay because its calmness belied hidden and treacherous reefs. She had to row around to the south side of the island and seek a concealed stone arch with one bright white stone among the grey. There she would have to row into the cave only when the tide was medium to low. She was told there was no other way to land.

'Great, huh Jack?'

He groaned as she rubbed his tummy.

She could probably fly, holding onto Jack but the whole idea was to keep a very low profile so as to be safe once she got there. If anyone saw a large winged creature, carrying a fully grown bloodhound, they'd think the pterodactyls had returned.

'Up ya get lazybones' she said to Jack, 'We need to find some food.'

They walked on a little while until Gabby stopped and sniffed the air. She smelled food, a pie maybe. She sniffed some more. Possibly a chicken she thought. She crouched down as she neared the top of a sand dune, Jack played along. Peeking over the rise between the tufts of crab grass she saw a young couple, maybe a little older than her and a middle aged woman. All were sitting on the back patio of a medium sized house.

She held Jack by the scruff of his neck.

'Could be a mother and children, Jack. What do you think?' she whispered in his ear. He licked her face and so she added,

'You're right, could be mother and child with significant other.'

She smiled, kissing the top of his mangy head. Hard to believe now, she thought, but she had been raised not to steal, to be compassionate and see the good in people. Well, the last two had gone out the window recently, and she doubted she could hang onto the do not steal bit much longer.

So she stood, tidied her hair as best she could, and

walked toward the young couple, the mother having gone inside. Jack by her side, she neared the gate to the property.

'Kate! Come. Eat!' A strong voice echoed from the house. The girl and boy stood. The boy glanced at Gabby and Jack, turned and walked inside with the girl. Gabby hesitated at the gate before noticing the chicken roasting on the spit.

The woman had mentioned food and Gabby was torn between doing the one thing she had just talked herself into not doing - stealing - or going hungry. A decision she ended up not having to make. Jack, on the other hand, had no such compunction. He jumped over the wall, took the chicken, spit and all, and bounded back over the stony wall and on down to the beach. Gabby ran after him.

She overtook the old bloodhound and chicken, running to the third currach, lifting up the end so both she and Jack could hide and eat in peace.

Gabby pulled off a leg and nearly swallowed it whole she was so hungry.

'Well, they had potatoes anyway so they won't be starving,' she said laughing, licking the sweet juices from her fingers and patting Jack on the head.

Fully sated and so tired, the two of them dozed off.

Gabby awoke with a start sitting up and banging her head on a seat of the overturned currach. She could hear talking coming from the beach and so, carefully raising an edge, she peeked out.

The mother and girl were fifty yards away scratching their heads and glancing up and down the beach. The young man was further away readying a small dinghy for sea. He had finished screwing the outboard to the stern and was now filling the tank with diesel.

Gabby lowered the currach once more. She had a plan, albeit an audacious one, but a plan nonetheless.

'Can you swim? Course you can,' she said looking at

the old bloodhound.

Peeking out from under the boat she saw that the women had gone back to the house. The twosome slid out and slithered up behind the second currach from the boy, and a minute later, the one closest to him. Gabby turned to Jack and whispered in his ear.

'Lead him! You must lead him away.' She gesticulated with her arm.

'God bless us, I must be mad,' she said crossing herself.

She watched him for several minutes more. He was going back and forth carrying boxes of supplies. As soon as he reached the top of the dune she pointed to Jack pushing him in the general direction she wanted him to run.

'Go Boy! Go!'

Off he ran howling at the sky, baying at imaginary wolves. Past the dinghy he went just as the young man reached the grass above the sand.

He stood transfixed for a couple of seconds before charging back down and along the beach.

'Stop, ya little gouger! Thieving mutt, come here!'

As man and dog headed further south along the shoreline Gabby ran down to the boat. Her adrenaline was pumping so hard as she tried to unknot the mooring rope that she didn't hear him return. Suddenly she felt him fling himself on top of her, pinning her arms and legs under him. In the distance Jack had run out of steam.

'Not only my dinner, but my boat as well ye little knacker!' he screamed in exasperation.

'Don't do this! I don't want to hurt you!' Gabby said, seething inside from being caught so easily.

'Hurt me? I think not,' he said, pinning her arms even harder into the sand.

Although on the verge of losing her temper, Gabby noticed what a good looking man he was with a mischievous grin, white teeth and strong tanned arms.

'It's not like we left you nothing. Didn't you have potatoes?' she asked.

He studied her beauty with the tousled red hair and greenest eyes.

'We managed!' he said, fascinated by this beauty beneath him.

'What is your name? Mine is Jones, Crabapple Jones, but most folks call me CJ.'

'Gabby' she smiled up at him.

'So, why did you steal my lunch . . . and nearly my boat?'

He stared hard into her eyes.

She is stunning he thought to himself. He eased up on her arms, but stayed sitting on her legs.

'Hungry! Okay? We were hungry, that's all. Get off me, will ye?' Gabby said, struggling to free herself.

'And the boat? Going to eat that too?' he said, pinning her down harder once more.

'I just needed to get to the other side of the bay to see my sick aunt. I was going to bring it back, I promise,' she whispered, subdued.

'All you had to do was ask,' he said letting her up. He glanced up at the house before ushering them into the boat.

'By the way, you were trying to undo the mooring,' he said pointing to where the rope was bound to a metal stake into the sand.

'This end is easier,' he said pulling on a knot at the bow of the boat.

As he turned to sit by the outboard he asked, 'Who's your aunt by the way . . .?'

That was the end of the conversation as she pushed him over the side, rushing to the engine and starting it up.

'Why you . . .' he said spluttering out some seawater.

'I'll bring it back, I promise,' she said, waving. Under

her breath she added, 'maybe next year.'

She gunned the engine and watched as he shook his head, bewildered, and strode up the dune.

A minute later, further down the beach, she heaved a tired and saturated Jack into the boat.

CHAPTER 9

The order is known as *The Monks of The Black Priory* but to the locals they were known as *The One Eyed Monks of Hell*. They are headquartered on the northern slopes of the western Pyrenees above San Sebastian in Spain. Their leader is feared far and wide as a dangerous psychopath, half Ukrainian, half Basque, known as Brother Visnik by the monks of the priory, and The Doctor by everyone else. Before his followers became monks they were usually orphans or children of poor families who could no longer afford to feed them.

Visnik controlled through a culture of fear. When his boys reached the age of eighteen one of their eyes was burned out by a hot poker. He gave them a choice: they could leave the Church and be hunted down and killed or they could pick which eye to lose. The hardest decision for many was which eye to choose.

Visnik reasoned that one good eye was to see the evil in people while the bad eye was to enable them to imagine the beauty of their god. It also made them better assassins because they learnt to heighten their other senses. None of this was particularly true. It just made him feel more powerful. It was all a myth. He had two good eyes himself. He'd read about a tribe in Africa doing the same thing as part of some obscure passage to manhood. He felt it might bond his disciples to him. It seemed to have worked well over the past thirty years.

The order still had some followers, mostly local lowlifes who had nowhere else to go. There were always one or two curious tourists hanging outside the gates hoping to catch a glimpse of the monks and their infamous leader. There was a service of sorts in the small chapel outside the gates, performed weekday evenings at six. The main reason for this was so they could continue the pretence of being a charity and keep their tax-free status.

Two days after the carnage at the campsite in Ireland, the Wednesday service had been completed with its usual congregation of waifs and strays. The monk who took the service was shaking the collection box at the back of the church. *Empty as usual*, he thought to himself.

As he lifted the swinging oak buttress into place he was startled by a raspy cough from behind. He let go of the log letting it slam back against the solid granite frame and turned around.

What an evil-looking woman, he thought to himself.

'Who let you in?' he stammered.

'Why, the good Lord, of course. You have a problem with that?' she said, soft spoken in the first the sentence but menacing in the second.

Brother Michael became wary. Nothing usually fazed him but there was something about the old crone that unnerved him. Regaining his composure he asked,

'Are you here for a confession of some kind?'

'Ha ha ha ha ha' she cackled. 'A confession? Ha ha ha, sonny boy, you'd be well dead by the time you heard my confession,' she said looking him up and down before turning and marching down the aisle toward the altar.

'So, what do you want?' he asked running after her.

'Visnik! Visnik is what I want. Go get him for me!' she

spat, facing him, her eyes burning into his. His skin whitened.

'And may I tell him who you are?'

She knelt down in front of the altar and whispered, 'No! He'll know.'

The monk hurried away as the woman leaned forward moving some lighted candles within easy reach. Returning her arms to her side she stared trancelike at the huge cracked stained glass window above her. There were many pieces missing, she noted, as the warm Saharan winds blew in through the gaps. After a few minutes of meditation she rolled up her sleeves and brought her arms over the candles, closer and closer to the flames until the sizzling of her flesh became audible. Two strong hands came over her shoulders and gently lifted her arms to safety.

'Scafa, Scafa, Scafa, why do you torture yourself so?' Visnik said pulling her to her feet and turning her to face him.

Visnik, at sixty, was still a striking figure. He bent forward and kissed her dry lips before leaning her head into his shoulder.

'Visnik, my love, you know why I do this. It's penance for my sins,' she said, before bursting into raucous laughter.

Visnik, grinning, nodded and said, 'You could be burnt at the stake twenty times and it would not be enough to forgive all your misdeeds, Scafa.'

'How kind to say that. Makes me feel better already' she said smiling.

Scafa was Gabby's great grandmother. It had been her grandson, the seventh son of the seventh son, who had raped Caitlan, Gabby's mother, at 'The Festival of Gypsies' in southern France. Scafa was the matriarch of a vast sprawling clan of Romany Gypsies that numbered in excess of twenty thousand people. They had their hand in every kind of criminal enterprise globally.

Visnik and Scafa had been lovers when he was a seventeen year old innocent living with his parents in the south of France and she was thirty eight and well on her way to becoming the leader of the Albanian/Romany clan known as the Menjaniis. She had taken him away, paid for medical school and set him up in the priory as a front for his and her illegal activities throughout Europe. Her empire was more mainstream crime, his was 'human resources' as he called it: mostly illegal body parts smuggling which made him enough money for his 'research'.

Although they still felt love for each other, the flames of passion had died long ago. She took his hand,

'Come sit with me and tell me the news.'

They sat in the front pew, still hand in hand. The old woman turned and faced her protégé.

'Any news from Ireland?'

Visnik knew he couldn't lie to her and so he replied,

'I haven't heard from them in three days . . . I'm sorry.'

She stood slowly facing him and slapped him so hard even the pigeons flew from their nests high in the rafters.

'You're sorry? Oh poor little boy, you're sorry? That's no answer! What happened?' The spittle flew from her twisted lips.

Visnik lifted his head and said, 'After our people destroyed everything and everyone at the campsite . . . '

'I know about the failure at the campsite. I'm talking about the Frenchman and that woman of his.'

'Well, er, from what I understand, they had the girl, Gabriella, drugged and in the van . . . '

'And?' she hissed.

'And, that's the last I heard. When my crew went to house there was no sign of them.' He sighed rubbing his face.

'So, the Frenchman called to say that they were bringing Gabriella here, that's all I know.' Visnik added.

'Didn't you . . . er . . . have a backup?' he asked, nervously knowing full well she had sent Stix.

Nobody ever questioned Scafa's motives about anything and lived to tell about it, except Visnik that is. He knew she'd not hurt him.

'Ha! I should have known you'd heard about Stix! One of my little rats squealing huh?' she spat. 'Not a word from him either.'

'Is it possible they have been arrested?' Scafa asked, sitting down beside him once more.

He glanced at her, 'I don't know. Anything's possible.'

'Ha, always the deep thinker you are. Of course, anything's possible!' She stood once more.

' Have you sent anyone?' she asked.

'Er, not yet, because they're partners, maybe they stopped somewhere for . . . ' She smacked him again, turned and walked back to the candles on the altar, sticking her hands right into the flames to stop her from killing him.

'Incompetent! That's what you are! You honestly think they might have stopped to have sex for a few days, while Gabriella was locked in the van? How stupid are you people?' she asked, removing her hands and dipping them in the font. Steam and the smell of burning flesh reaching his nostrils. He didn't react. He knew better.

'Send someone to look for them!' she said 'Now!'

He jumped to his feet and rushed into the rectory.

Scafa sat once more, a few tears leaking down her face. Not because of the physical pain, more an emotional one for the weakness and indecision in the boy she'd loved so much, a long time ago.

CHAPTER 10

Philippe and Sheila had been sheltering in a ruined barn on the outskirts of Galway city for the past three days. He had gone into the city every day for food and any off-the-shelf medicines he thought might help Sheila get over the pain of having her hand severed. Her hearing and sight were returning slowly but the fever she'd been suffering had barely diminished.

In the city he'd also bought a tent, sleeping bags, disposable mobile phones and a small portable gas stove. All in all, they were in the best place to be. They couldn't risk a hospital or doctor - too many questions - nor could they attempt to travel back to France - way too risky for two reasons. One, Philippe might get through security but Sheila wouldn't, at least, not in her present condition. Two, Visnik would probably kill them both for failing their mission. They reasoned the only way to survive was to find the girl and bring her back to the priory.

Two days later Sheila's fever broke and with a new dressing she seemed comfortable enough to travel. They took the Clifden bus from Galway's city centre, arriving back in the fishing hamlet of Cleggan several days after their initial encounter with the girl there.

Philippe installed Sheila in a house similar to the one he'd broken into the week before. They had grown closer in the time they had spent together, mainly because they had never spent so much time on a job. He liked that. He kissed her on the lips before asking her to contact someone 'safe' at the priory and track the GPS left on the dog. They had lost all their equipment when they'd lost the van.

On a reconnoitre of the village he'd asked several people about the girl and dog and had been lucky to find a farmer who'd seen them but disappointed to learn he'd only pointed them in the direction of the ferries. They could be anywhere. There were hundreds of islands off the coast of Connemara. Over twenty of them had thriving communities; others were still inhabited by old family estates. More again had summer homes bought by the 'Dublin Crowd' as the locals referred to the nouveaux riche of Ireland. Some islands had abandoned mansions, churches and monasteries from long times past.

Philippe entered the house somewhat defeated by what he had learned. Sheila on the other hand was animated as she hung up the phone.

'I just spoke to the Priory. They have tracked the dog to Clifden, so our chances are looking better' she said smiling.

'Ah oui. That is good news,' he said.

He knew he was falling for her but in his practical mind he knew he couldn't afford to progress further, at least not until the job was completed.

Philippe and Sheila were both excellent killers. They had been trained from an early age to use every kind of weapon imaginable: from guns to knives, from bows to bazookas. But in all the years of killing they'd never encountered anything like Gabby.

Sheila added, 'All Visnik had said was to be prepared for anything. She might be dangerous.'

'Hah! Might be dangerous!' Philippe said out loud, causing Sheila a look of puzzlement and then a nod of understanding.

'How about the fact she could fly, or have daggers growing out of her fingers?'

Sheila came up behind him and wrapped her good arm around his shoulder, softly kissing his neck.

'Don't worry, we'll get her, chérie,' she said as he moved away trying to keep his mind focused.

Their guns had been destroyed by the girl and so they improvised. Sheila gave the Frenchman two aerosol cans of deodorant and a lighter she'd found around the house which should work as mini flamethrowers. Philippe had found gutting, hunting and carving knives. He gave the carving knives to Sheila.

With her hand firmly wrapped they boarded the bus to Clifden. They both admitted it might be a wild goose chase because the dog might never have hooked up with the girl at all. He could have just wandered off or been taken by someone else. Still, they decided to check it out as there were no other leads as to her whereabouts.

Two hours later, with the help of the communication centre at the Priory in Spain, they had pinpointed the GPS signal. They found it on an idling tractor trailer at the local abattoir. Due to Sheila's limited dexterity, Philippe had to be the one to comb through the cow crap to locate the locator. He wasn't happy about that.

'I was sure she had taken a boat somewhere and after this, ...this merde, now I am certain,' he said, more to himself than her, as they walked back to the bus stop.

It upset him even more to discover there wasn't another bus until morning. They could well afford the best hotel but reasoned the sleaziest B and B would be a safer bet rather than risk attention trying to hitchhike. They found one in an alleyway at the back of Market Street.

Their search would wait another day. Sheila's arm, on the other hand, could not. The stump had begun to smell.

CHAPTER 11

Gabriella and Jack had been motoring towards the main inhabited island of Inishbofin. They were reaching the end of the bay and out of its protection from the stormy Atlantic rollers.

Meanwhile, Crabapple Jones was drowning his sorrows in Oliver's pub after losing his boat to the girl. His mother had been very upset, to put it mildly, and had threatened to throw him out of the house. His self pity and fuming were interrupted by the laughter of some fishermen he didn't recognise.

'Ah sure, she'll be floatin' out in the bay by morning' one said. 'Exhausted and half dead I'll say.'

The other one agreed.

Jones stood and walked over to them.

'You talking about the girl in the dinghy?' he asked.

'Did she leave you, your love? Ha ha ha' the first one said.

CJ pulled a filleting knife from his belt and laid it against the man's throat.

'I'll ask you again, who are you talking about?'

The other one stepped back, raising his arms in the air in mock surrender.

'A shark you ejiit, a feckin basking shark.'

The young man stepped away, lowering the knife to his side, but keeping it close just in case these men had other ideas.

'Sorry about that. Let me ask you, why would a basking shark be nearly dead by morning?'

The two looked at each other, the leader shrugged.

'Simple, we got a 'poon in her with twenty yards of cable attached to an oil drum. Nothing could pull on that all night. Except your girlfriend maybe, ha ha ha.'

Jones felt anger welling up in him and swung at the nearest of the two knocking him flying over a table and onto the floor. He stormed out of the pub and ran to the pier. His biggest concern wasn't so much the girl, it was his boat. These idiots had left probably a two inch thick cable strung out somewhere in the bay. For the bigger boats it would be no problem. They'd pick it up on sonar, but for a small boat with no sonar and fading light and a wounded shark, anything could happen.

He ran down to the jetty, waving and pointing at the currach with outboard and at Festy O'Neil up on the dock.

'Hey Festy, twenty minutes okay?'

The old man nodded. In one smooth motion CJ untied the painter, pushed and leapt into the boat. He had the engine started before the bow left the concrete slip and was heading toward open sea in seconds.

Gabby had just reached the open sea when the engine started to hesitate. The undulating waves were not large yet, but further out, she could see the white froth blowing off their crests. Gabby had grown up afraid of nothing, but the task in front of her was a daunting one. The little outboard motor spluttered and died.

Growing up in campsites and trailer parks she knew a

little about of the intricacies of engines and she reasoned an engine was an engine whether it be marine or land based. She stood and gave the starter chord a few pulls, nothing happened. Just as she was about to sit down once more the boat lifted several feet throwing her against the engine cowling and splitting her forehead above her left eye. As the dinghy settled back into the water a giant shape materialized on the starboard side, its massive tail beating the water alongside.

There was an eerie sound of screeching metal against metal. Gabby rubbed her head. The bleeding was not severe enough to warrant any further worry. She had other things to deal with. She told Jack not to panic and then dunked her head below the outboard into the freezing Atlantic water.

Once her head was submerged she could see the problem. The huge fish was in the throes of death. A harpoon was stuck in its head above the eye and in its panic the steel cable had become wrapped several times around its flukes. Gabby was a fast learner and in her short life had read every book she could lay her hands on, the favourites, by far, being about the natural world.

She immediately knew that it was a basking shark, a normally giant docile creature of the deep, that had been hunted down and left to die. Apart from the crushing cable she knew it couldn't feed itself on the millions of krill it needed to sustain its massive size.

She pulled her head out of the water and was shaking the cold droplets from her hair when suddenly Jack was standing, front paws on the gunwale, barking in the opposite direction from where the shark was. She rubbed the water from her eyes and stared into the gloom of dusk. At first she didn't see it but then with eyes dried she focused and saw a large black barrel heading for the boat.

With the cable snagged under her propeller, she understood immediately the reason the shark was so exhausted. She reached under the engine once more and tried to remove the slow moving cable. At one point she nearly had it until an unravelling piece of metal pierced her hand causing the most terrible pain. She knew the only way to stop her hand being ripped off was to go into the water and keep it level. She took a deep breath and over the side she went.

Swimming alongside the cable she concentrated hard and her finger talons extended. She made quick work of the strand of cable before kicking hard toward the shark. Unfortunately the shark was not quite finished struggling and when it saw Gabby closing in it gave one last pull with its huge fins and tail causing the ripple effect underwater to halt her progress for precious seconds.

This final surge moved the barrel on the surface closer and closer to the little boat. Jack barked once and hunkered down in the bow as the oil drum struck the motor, pulling it off the boat and causing some of the planks to crack. Trickles of water started appearing inside the boat, Jack barked louder.

Meanwhile, a mile away Crabapple Jones scanned the bay with his binoculars. He knew there was no 'sick aunt' but had no clue as to where Gabby was going and why. If she wanted one of the larger islands a ferry would be more practical, so therefore, she was desperate to get to a smaller one. *Which one and why?* he asked himself.

The bay was calm now and so sounds travelled much greater distances. He pricked up his ears at the noise of metal striking metal.

'There!' he said out loud spotting something in the water far out of the bay. By the time he'd adjusted his course there was nothing there to see. *Now I'm hearing things*.

Gabby surfaced. Sucking in some air and quickly reassuring Jack she'd be there soon, she dived once more until she held the cable strangling the mighty shark. With all talons extended, she made quick work of cutting through the cables wrapping the beast's giant frame. All that was left was the large barbed hook above its eye. She severed the hook as close as she dare to the barb without losing too much of the fish's flesh. Then she kicked hard for the surface.

After several deep breaths of air she spotted the sinking boat and howling old dog twenty feet away. She knew she had only one option. She hadn't needed to deploy her wings, and didn't even know if they would be a help or hindrance under the sea, but she knew she needed to try them now.

Half a mile away CJ was about to give up on his boat and the girl when he was suddenly distracted by something he was sure was impossible. He cut the engine and stood transfixed peering through his binoculars. He thought he saw a huge bird picking up a dog and flying away. He sat down, then turned the engine back on and headed for the spot he thought he'd seen this miraculous vision.

'Drink, must be the drink,' he said out loud, steering seaward while scratching his head. He needed his boat back.

CHAPTER 12

Philippe and Sheila arrived back in Cleggan the next day. Into Oliver's they went for some early lunch. Sean, the barman, was a jovial enough sort and spouted forth all kinds of news and gossip from the night before. The killers were well used to playing the innocents abroad routine and so with the unsuspecting Sean, they did just that.

'So tell me Sean, is there a vet around here? Our dog is not well,' Sheila asked with concern.

'Ah sorry to hear that, em, there are two in the area alright, but you'd be wanting Petey. He's just up the road a bit.'

'Something wrong with the other one?' Philippe asked brusquely, playing a mind game he was so good at.

Sean leaned on the bar and said, irritated,

'Nothing wrong, just doubt you two could find her!'

'Is this a gender thing?' Sheila inquired, touching the Frenchman's leg below the bar.

'Huh?' Sean asked slightly taken aback.

'Well, maybe you've a thing about independent women, so you refer anyone who asks to 'Petey' is that it?' Philippe said, without emotion.

'Yeah, telling them they'll never find her place, is that

it?' Women have no place in your small-minded, male-dominated world, huh?' Sheila asked, winking as Sean turned his head in disbelief.

Sean, hands on the bar in front of him, stretched to full height,

'The reason, you little shite, is that Jane Stephens, the vet, lives way out of town, a hard place for anyone to find, below the Diamond. That's a mountain in Letterfrack, okay?' he said, slamming his fist down on the counter as if to reinforce his point.

Sheila and the Frenchman paid for their food and hurried out the door muttering 'Thank yous.' Sean just stood there not quite sure what had just taken place. Outside, the two assassins chuckled to themselves while removing their disguises. Philippe had a false moustache and a long black wig over his hairless pate while Sheila had a blonde wig and light blue contacts. They needed a vet in a remote area and now they knew where one was to be found.

Jane Stephens was a widowed mother in her fifties. She was self-absorbed, opinionated and rude, but an excellent veterinary surgeon according to all who knew her. She'd lived in Connemara all her life. Her father had been the only vet for a hundred miles during and after the Second World War.

Her husband had died twenty years ago, having been gored to death by a Hereford bull. The inquest had ruled death by misadventure. Jane had said they were idiots and held the bull's owner responsible for being careless in not securing the animal properly for examination.

Years later she'd got her revenge on that farmer by reporting his cruelty of animals to the authorities. The man had lost his business and died penniless of alcoholism. She never gloated about what she'd done. She reasoned to herself that that's just the way it should be.

Jane was out back in the yard feeding the hens, when she heard a car pull up on her gravel driveway. Never one to rush, she knew most people would find her if they needed to, otherwise they could wait.

After ten minutes had passed with no sign of anyone, she decided she'd better go check things out. Before entering the house she noticed Paddy Whelan's car. 'Strange' she muttered to herself, knowing Paddy had set sail a few weeks before toward Iceland and Greenland 'for a wee bit of explorin', as he had put it.

In the mudroom inside the back door there was a closet in which she kept a couple of her dad's shotguns. With eyes peeled she snuck inside the house and opened the well-oiled closet door. She was proud of herself for maintaining her home as well as her father had. The guns were gone, both of them. Now she was scared.

As she turned to leave the house once more a man stepped out from behind her neatly trimmed hedge. He pointed her shotgun,

'If you please Madame, go into the kitchen and I will not hurt you.'

He sounded French to Jane. As she passed through the swing door to the kitchen she swung it hard behind her, but Philippe was too clever to fall for that one and so she began to run but unfortunately there was a woman sitting in the breakfast nook holding the other gun, finger on the trigger, leaning it on a blood-soaked towel where her hand should be.

Philippe waited patiently as the door stopped swinging, then with the barrel of the shotgun he pushed it open and joined the women by the window.

'Madame, we need your help and for this we will pay you well,' he said pointing for her to sit. Jane sat, crossed her arms over her chest like a child unwilling to comply.

'Pointing my own guns at me is an unusual way to ask for help. Is that how the French do it?' Jane said, scornfully.

'We will do whatever is necessary. We can be civil or not. It's up to you, Madame,' Philippe said, with malevolent eyes.

Jane shrugged her shoulders and asked,

'I presume you need me to do something with that?' she asked, nodding her head toward Sheila's arm.

'Show her!'

He held his gun tight from across the room, making sure he could cover all angles. Sheila slipped off the wet towel. Her stump oozed thick coagulated blood onto the floor. The skin around it was odorous, red and inflamed.

'Well, I don't know what I can do,' Jane said, leaning forward examining the wound.

'Looks to me like you're in need of a doctor,' she said matter-of-factly.

Before Jane knew it the barrel of her shotgun was pressed firmly against the back of her neck.

'Just do what you can,' Philippe said angrily.

Jane had little choice but to comply. They all traipsed into the surgery where Sheila lay down on the steel bed. Philippe stood by the door, shotgun raised. Jane hummed out loud as she efficiently moved around the room, opening and closing cabinets, checking bottle labels, rattling drawers full of shiny surgical instruments. She eyed the clock, checking the time every so often was crucial for her plan to work.

With the unwieldy gun in his hands, Philippe couldn't risk getting too close and so decided that there had to be some modicum of trust between them. Jane was moving so quickly with the glass vials and syringes that even an alert Sheila had difficulty following her movements.

'Okay, I have here a shot of morphine and a shot of Pentothal to knock you out, you ready?' she asked.

'The other one is what?' asked Philippe pointing to the third syringe.

'That's a strong antibiotic I'll administer at the end . . . okay?'

He nodded. There were also scalpels, horse needles and cat gut to sew up the skin.

At five minutes to twelve, exactly, the tip of a beak could be seen unzipping the cloth covering the five foot tall standing birdcage in the living room. Neither Sheila nor Philippe had paid it any attention when entering the house.

In the surgery, Jane was tying off the last of the stitches on the stump of the unconscious woman. It was now one minute to twelve.

As she lifted the last syringe Philippe moved forward.

'Show me the bottle this comes from please,' he said.

Jane turned, hiding the panic from her face and the trembling in her body, knowing full well it was insulin in the needle that it would kill the woman.

At twelve o'clock on the dot there was the sound of a door slamming and heavy clumping feet walking across the living room floor.

'Where's me lunch, woman?' came the bellowing voice.

It distracted Philippe enough that Jane could ask one quick question shaking Sheila awake.

'Who are you after?'

The Pentothal, painkiller and truth serum, worked.

'The girl, Gabriella,' was all she said.

Philippe grabbed Jane by the hair and whispered intently,

'Who's that?'

Jane held up the syringe and said,

'My boyfriend. Let me do this and I'll get rid of him.'

Before Philippe had a chance to react, Jane plunged the insulin into the woman's arm and turned for the door. The Frenchman held her arm, not sure what to do. He was concerned about Sheila but more so about the man in the kitchen. He didn't want to kill the two of them. Such an absence would surely lead to a manhunt and little chance of finding the girl.

The sound of pounding fists on a table from the other room made his mind up for him.

'I give you one minute to get rid of him otherwise you both die, vous comprenez?' he spat.

Jane nodded and removing her blood splattered apron, she left the room.

Philippe went over to Sheila's side .Lifting her hand, he said,

'All done chérie, you can wake up now.'

Nothing, no movement.

Jane quickly walked through the house picking Henry up in her right hand as she rushed out of the rear door. Once outside she threw him up in the air saying,

'Adventure, Henry, adventure!'

The white cockatoo flapped its wings and mimicked,

'Adventure, adventure, Henry's having an adventure!'

Jane had adopted Henry and his sister, Perdita, many years prior from an elderly woman whose husband had died when he fell in a ditch on the way home from the pub. He'd been a nasty specimen of humanity, she felt, but she couldn't blame the birds and so Jane had been happy to take them on. They'd had many years of laughter and frustration since. Perdita lived with her daughter, Maureen.

Meanwhile, in the surgery, Philippe was becoming increasingly concerned by Sheila's lack of movement. Finally he'd lifted her hand and checked for a pulse. There was none. He turned and bolted into the living room.

Outside Jane ran into the horse barn and leapt onto the seat of her quad bike. She pressed the starter a couple of times, held in the clutch, into first gear, released and off they went out through the rear of the stables.

'Hi Ho Silver!' shrieked Henry as they tore off down the track.

CHAPTER 13

Scafa's home in southern France was a far cry from her meagre beginnings in the pre World War Two campsites of the Wallachia region of south western Romania.

Her life was a compilation of cruelty and unspeakable horror. Some was inflicted upon her while she did her fair share to others. Born in 1932, at the ripe old age of eight she had been arrested for shoplifting. *Later her father beat her.* At nine, she went back to the same place and stuck a kitchen knife into the shopkeeper. *Later her father beat her.* At eleven, she tortured her sister's pet dog by cutting off an ear. *Later her father beat her.* At twelve, her father's brother tried to molest her and she stuck her finger into his eye, removing it from the socket. *That night her father beat her severely.*

A week later she poured three bottles of 100 percent illicit alcohol on her father and set fire to it.

He never beat her again. He never did anything again.

At fifteen, she had sex with a cousin and later gave birth to her first son. Every two years thereafter she gave birth to all male children: seven sons. It didn't matter to her who the fathers were. At twenty seven, she decided she had had enough. She had had a master plan all her life and her seventh son was only a player in the grand scheme of things.

She arranged for number seven, Tobias, to marry his first cousin, Elana, on his sixteenth birthday. She was a little older but of good stock. Scafa made sure of that. As Tobias and Elana's family grew, members of the Menjanii clan of travellers and thieves, cutthroats and criminals, began to respect Scafa enough that, at thirty-eight, she was voted the leader of their Romany clan.

The suspicion and envy surrounding Scafa increased as Tobias sired his fifth son in a row. Scafa had bodyguards, but even they were no match for her skill in unarmed combat, shooting, knife fighting and throwing. The woman had been training herself since birth.

She had been certain since her first son was born, that there would be a seventh son of a seventh son. He who would rule the clan and spread fear around the world, more than the Triads, the Yakusa and even the Mafia.

She was convinced it was her destiny. That was until her idiot grandson, Malut, the seventh, had raped the Irish girl who'd then had a daughter. He'd been murdered by the girl's father. Revenge now was all she sought in life.

It was time now to go and find the girl. She no longer had any confidence in Visnik or anyone else. After washing and dressing, she went to a huge oak armoire concealed behind the rows of clothes. She opened a large drawer and flipped through several passports from many countries.

They all seemed to show pictures of different women but, in fact, it was the same woman. Scafa had mastered the art of disguise since arrest warrants had been issued by Interpol for her over the years. Seven warrants for murder. In addition, numerous warrants had been issued by the FBI for money laundering, prostitution, sex and drug trafficking, attempted murder, grievous bodily harm.

The list went on and on.

She picked the same passport she had used last time to see Visnik in Spain. She knew she didn't need one but liked to carry it in case she was stopped and questioned. If she had no ID the chances were they would detain her until they found out who she was. That would be too late.

She opened the drawer beneath and rolled up her left sleeve until tight on her bicep. She lifted out her 'pin pusher' as she loved to call it.

Years ago while in a pub in the Ukraine some of the Romanies were getting very drunk and were playing the game of throwing tiny arrows into a corkboard circle of numbers. She found out later it was called darts. Anyway, one of these darts skidded off the metal frame and stuck in Scafa's leg. At first she was angry but, on removing it, she came up with an idea for a cunning weapon.

She had returned to Bucharest and visited with a trusted family friend. He was a jeweller by trade but at that time he had fingers in many pies. She told him what she wanted him to make and three weeks later went back to his little shop. He produced for her what looked like a large chunky arm bracelet. Before picking it up she thought it would be way too heavy for her forearm to bear. But when she lifted it up, she was surprised to find that he'd made it of gold plate and it was light. She managed to clasp it together easily without pinching her skin. The top looked like uneven rolled gold while the inside was smooth.

There were two tiny clasps holding secret compartments which were easy to unhook when holding her arm vertically. Inside the larger one were twenty spring-loaded tungsten darts approximately four inches in length. They were naturally the colour of grey steel. The smaller compartment held only six darts but they were very special. Scafa lifted one out, carefully releasing the spring loader, and examined it closely. There were two tiny holes right at the tip to hold the poison.

When he had told her what kind of poison he had

obtained for them Scafa had laughed and laughed so much she thought she might have a heart attack. The poison was from the Columbian Golden Poison Dart Frog. *How appropriate* she thought. It was one of the rarest and deadliest poisons in the world and extremely difficult to obtain. Hence only six darts were contained in the smaller compartment. With the precise skill of a master watchmaker, the intricate mechanism had been so perfectly tuned she could shoot off one dart or all in sequence. The manner in which she accomplished this was devised during a visit to a seedy free clinic on the docks in Marseilles, France.

Doctor Antione Sousa was not a trusted friend of the Romanies. But Scafa needed his skill and knowledge of mechanics and the human body. He had once been a highly respected transplant surgeon until he'd got an underage girl pregnant and accidently killed her during an abortion. Nobody actually knew if it had been an accident but Scafa had always had her doubts. After all, he was married with four children already.

He spliced the tendon from her left index finger and inserted a minute 'booster' implant. Thus, Scafa was able to manoeuvre the tiny shooting instrument strapped to her lower arm hidden in the bracelet.

Her surgery had been long and intricate, the healing and learning process even longer, but it had worked. When attaching the device she merely had to plug it in to a tiny socket in the epidermis above the wrist.

When all was completed, Sousa and Scafa wanted to test the device. They decided to take a stroll through the Marseilles dock land, knowing they would come across an involuntary participant with ease. They found a filthy old man sleeping under the pilings.

They roused him and he struggled to his feet making a threatening gesture toward them. Scafa shot him through the sternum. He keeled over, frothing from his mouth, having no clue as to what had happened to him. Sousa ripped open his foul smelling clothes and tried to find the tiny pinprick in his chest. It was invisible to the naked eye.

Back outside the clinic, Scafa paid the doctor and headed back to her fortress outside Grasse, in the Provence region of France, to fully recuperate.

CHAPTER 14

Although nearly dark, Gabby's incredible ability to see since her transformation made the landing much smoother for her and Jack.

The take-off had been a struggle for her, carrying the dead weight of a fully grown bloodhound. But once they had reached a safe altitude of two hundred feet, it had all gone well. On realizing where he was, Jack had started yelping like a puppy again but was easily soothed by Gabby's soft voice in his ears.

However, after a few miles of smooth flight, she began to tire. Her wings hadn't reached full length yet and the muscles supporting them weren't fully developed. They began to sag which caused a loss of height.

Gabby could see the south tip of Inishbofin Island off in the haze of darkness and so she made a decision. She partially lowered her wings to give herself a little energy boost when it came to the final push. Jack thought this wasn't fun anymore and started howling at the rapidly approaching sea below. Ten feet above the waves, Gabby pulled back her huge wings and with powerful thrusting strokes she soared upwards once more.

At over a thousand feet she ran out of strength but

managed to keep her wings level, thus enabling her to glide gently on the cool Atlantic breeze toward Inishbofin.

Upon landing she checked around the isolated area of the still inhabited island and, once sure of their safety, she retracted her wings back into her body. She quickly pulled on the jacket she'd carried with Jack and hunkered down with her companion in a small sheltered rock crevice above the churning sea. There they slept.

Back at the vet's house Philippe had finished feeling sorry for himself and the loss of his beloved co-conspirator. He quickly lifted her body placing it gently in the boot, packed the guns and extra shells into the stolen car, stopping only briefly to grab some food from the fridge. He decided there was no point in trying to track the vet. She'd gone down what was more like a trail rather than a road and he couldn't risk getting stuck out in the middle of nowhere.

He snickered to himself.

'This whole place is the middle of nowhere.'

He drove the back roads to Cleggan, reasoning it was the last place the girl had been seen by anybody.

Gabby was awakened by Jack's slobbery kisses all over her face. She gently pushed him away only to have him return, twice as doggedly, to try to lick her to death.

'Jack! Stop it!' she cried with no real conviction pulling him onto the grass with her.

As she rubbed his tummy she surveyed the land around her looking for any signs of civilization. There was a ruined church off in the distance but she saw no sign of either tourists or locals.

She unfurled her wings to see if she had any strength left. Surprisingly she felt no pain and they seemed to beat stronger than ever. They were both hungry now and so she decided it was more prudent to continue toward Kelly's Island and risk being seen than staying on the island for the day and risk being discovered.

She tied her windbreaker around Jack's middle, using the sleeves. Jack looked at the jacket then at Gabby and knowingly started to howl as she picked him up with both arms while running toward the cliff edge high above the ocean. Just as she leapt off the precipice her beautiful wings tilted down slightly and started to beat keeping them safely above the rocks below.

Scanning the island and sea she started her climb to a safer altitude just below the low cumulus clouds. There was little or no air traffic in these parts except the high contrails of planes heading across the Atlantic to America or the occasional search and rescue helicopter.

Even flying against the gentle western breeze, Gabby was feeling confident enough in her strength to climb into the cotton ball clouds and then glide back down to view the ocean below. After the first couple of times Jack began to enjoy this new game and howled appreciatively.

Binky McFarland had a severe hangover on this particular morning. He'd successfully flown his hang glider from the tip of Cornwall, in England, to Ennis, County Clare, Ireland. The welcoming committee made up of friends from both countries had celebrated his achievement until four o'clock that morning.

That had been the first stage of his journey around the islands of Britain and Ireland and he swore to himself, because of the way he felt, that the next celebration should be at the completion of the whole trip, rather than after every stage of it.

Binky had taken off from The Cliffs of Moher, County Clare four hours ago on the way to Achill Island, seventy miles north. His custom lawn mower engine putted along at up to twenty mph below the twenty foot fabric wings, enabling him to stay high above the waves and farmlands below.

Binky's hoverglider, *ultralight*, as he called it, was

equipped with GPS positioning and a short wave radio. He didn't have any kind of sonar or radar device because he kept under the clouds. Binky was feeling a bit dopey at this stage and wasn't paying much attention to his altimeter as he flew into the clouds and back out again.

Then the inevitable happened, both girl and dog and man and machine exited the clouds simultaneously.

Talk about seeing pink elephants, Binky thought to himself. He was looking at a flying girl carrying what looked to him like a bloodhound. Anyway, it didn't matter then as her brilliant feathered wing sliced clean through the canopy above his head, causing him to spiral out of control toward the sea below.

It took Gabby only seconds to realize what had just taken place. Without hesitation she moved Jack under her left arm, pulled in her wings and dropped like a stone toward the screaming man in the damaged ultralight.

Binky knew he was in serious trouble as he plummeted downward.

He got on the radio and shouted,

'Mayday, Mayday,' and repeated his co ordinates several times.

At the speed he was falling he knew there was little chance of survival upon hitting the ocean. He glanced down at the altimeter, 100 . . . 80 . . . 50 . . . 20 . . . and was bracing himself for impact when suddenly he stopped falling.

Gabby reached down and grasped the aluminium strut of the glider. With wings now fully deployed she wasn't sure if she had the strength to complete what she was attempting.

She did.

Binky looked up in amazement at the stunning creature now gently lowering him to the water.

'Undo your safety harness,' she said.

'Huh?' was all he could say.

'Undo your seat belt and inflate your life vest . . . now!'

Gabby shouted, knowing he was suffering severe shock.

It worked as Binky released his harness and floated onto the sea. Gabby let go, once again holding Jack with both arms.

'Are you going to be alright?' she asked.

'I think so, what . . . .who are you?' he asked nervously.

Gabby reversed her wings, beating them slowly backwards as she hovered a few feet from the floating man. She studied him hard before answering.

'I'm just a girl, an unusual one, but basically, I'm just a girl.'

Binky's homing device was flashing and beeping on his life vest and Gabby knew she had to go.

Moving further and further backwards he watched her in absolute awe.

'Thank you, thank you, I'll never tell another soul what happened here today. I promise.'

She stared a little longer before giving him a wink and a wave as she turned, propelling herself high into the air once more.

Binky watched her for several minutes, a tear running down his cheek, sure he would never see such a beautiful creature again.

CHAPTER 15

Visnik drove his black Hummer down the dirt road in southern France. He'd been summoned by Scafa and he wasn't happy. Nobody summoned Visnik, especially a woman, but this particular woman was different. He was scared of her.

The only sign that there was a house out here was a weathered old open gate, now miles behind, with a faded yellow bolt of lightning painted on it. No words, no name, nothing to signify the existence of her home he was now approaching.

He knew Scafa's mind. It was a tease, daring anyone to come onto her substantial property: thirty thousand acres of woods and streams. There was every kind of hidden security all around the house and grounds. Claymore mines nailed to trees with tripwires to shred anything that set them off, cameras, regular and thermal imaging, motion detectors, everything to keep her safe. She treasured her privacy and security.

Scafa had told him to obey the road signs no matter what. There hadn't been any until now. He came upon a lone dilapidated STOP sign two hundred yards from the house. It was right at the end of the driveway he'd been on for ten minutes now. He stopped and a camera came up out of the ground in tandem with a twenty foot long solid steel ramp about four feet tall blocking his path. He pressed the intercom and after a minute the ramp and camera withdrew back into the earth. The only words spoken were,

'Stay in the car when reaching the door.'

On closer inspection the large house looked like a ruin. The tiles on the roof were askew with some missing. The chimney was leaning. Some of the glass seemed to be missing from the windows. The grey aged teak siding was, in many places, popping and cracked. The double hung front doors were the same faded red as the stop sign.

'What a dump,' Visnik said to himself.

He was about to open the car door when a golden retriever came from the side of the house and sat ten feet in front of the vehicle. It stared at Visnik for several minutes. Visnik stared back at the harmless-looking mutt.

Then the dog barked a couple of times. Visnik was about to think the whole exercise was a waste of time, when suddenly he spotted several dark shadows moving threateningly around his car. He leaned forward to get a better look from his side mirrors and saw three, no four, Rottweilers sniffing the tyres. Several more minutes passed before all five dogs retreated out of sight behind the home, as if to some hidden signal.

Visnik gingerly got out of the car as the main door to the house opened soundlessly. Scafa herself beckoned him forward. He then noticed the steel lining on the inside of the wooden doors.

'Special titanium and Kevlar alloy. Will stop an RPG or fifty calibre bullet at close range. Come inside,' she said.

Expecting to see a dusty old mausoleum styled interior he was astounded at the modern crispness that confronted him. The house was tastefully decorated with all the up-to-date gadgets of life in the twenty-first century.

'Incredible,' was all he could say.

Even the windows that looked broken from the outside were, in fact, complete units of, he guessed, three inch thick bullet proof glass.

Scafa rapped on the wall with her cane causing the unmistakable sound of metal to resonate throughout the room. She pointed to a coffee table laid out with the finest china.

'Sit' she said, taking her place on the couch opposite.

'So my friend, any news?' she inquired politely.

Visnik sipped the coffee and looked deep into the woman's eyes. He seriously resented the summons but after some consideration had concluded she was right to be mad at him. His people had so far failed.

'The Irish authorities have found a body, outside a village where the girl was last seen,' said Visnik, without much enthusiasm.

'A body? How exciting! Now pray tell me you know who it is, this body,' she asked, dripping in sarcasm.

Before answering, Visnik pondered the question a little too long.

'Well?' she spat.

'Yes, yes, sorry er, it was the body of a vet we think, but it could have been the body of Philippe's associate. We just don't know yet.'

'And this body stands out to you, why?'

'Because murders in the west of Ireland are extremely rare and after the fiasco at the campsite I'm sure it's somehow connected.' he said.

'Hmm, quite the deep thinker you are,' she said with little emotion.

'Now, just you wait a minute! I haven't driven through the night to put up with your crass innuendos and sarcastic insinuations.' Visnik rose from his chair.

Scafa looked him up and down remembering the passion they had shared a long time ago.

'I'm sorry. We need to find this child, quickly, before she gets too strong. Please sit and give me some idea of what your plans might be.'

Visnik sat down and they discussed their options. Finally past midnight they decided they should go to Ireland themselves and finish it.

CHAPTER 16

After saving the man in the ultralight, Gabby continued on toward Kelly's Island. But her strength was fading once more. They were only a few feet above the waves and she was fading fast. She knew she had screwed up in so many ways. Knowing her wings weren't strong enough for everything she had put them through she had blindly continued on and on and now she could fly no more.

'What an ending, I'm sorry Jack,' she whispered as she hit the cold Atlantic sea.

Gabby didn't even have the strength to retract her wings and so she lay there on her back bobbing like a cork on the undulating ocean waves. She patted her tummy for Jack to climb on and after a few minutes he relented and did so gingerly. Gabby felt sad at her predicament and a bit sorry for herself. She rolled back over until her mouth was inches from the sea. She let out a piercing shriek while ducking her head under the water to try and revive herself.

She focused her eyes once more. There was something large and black moving slowly toward her. She shook the hair of her face just as the giant basking shark surfaced beside her. She felt no panic only hope as she was awed by the beauty of one of nature's most misunderstood creatures.

The shark slid under her, lifting Gabby and Jack on its back and well out of the icy cold ocean. There the giant beast stayed, basking in the sunlight, keeping its cargo dry.

Three hours in the sun, lying on the back of the shark, rejuvenated Gabby and Jack to such an extent that both girl and canine stood up on the barnacle incrusted behemoth. Gabby told Jack to wait as she took off into the wind soaring effortlessly while testing her body's strength. She felt very alive once more and with minimal effort plucked Jack off the sharks back. She hovered briefly above the great beast's head, mouthing the words, 'Thank you' before pumping her wings once more toward the skies. The huge shark flicked its tail and dived back to the depths below.

Two hours later Gabby circled Kelly's island. From the air, the island looked unspoiled and safe. She saw trees and plants she'd only read about in school, normally seen on tropical islands, not here, off the coast of Ireland.

She landed softly in a clearing, lowering Jack first on a mossy hillock. He was happy to be back on dry ground, running and barking and peeing everywhere like a newborn pup.

Gabby sat on a log and retracted her tired wings, pulling her jacket around her. She was very, very tired after all that had taken place in the few days since that terrible night in the campsite.

But she knew she couldn't relax yet. She had to see this friend of her mother's, this Mo Mo Kelly, first and decide if she was really in a safe place or not. But it was not to be, her eyelids grew heavier and heavier. Within minutes she was fast asleep, Jack plonked down beside her, exhausted.

Sometime later she felt Jack's wet tongue on her face and so without opening her eyes she pushed him away.

'Go back to sleep,' she said, stifling a yawn.

Before she knew it he started barking. She opened one eye to berate him further but the look on his face stopped her. Jack was staring at something behind and above her. She rolled over slowly. She couldn't quite make out what it was because of her sleepy eyes and the descending sun behind it.

Gabby sat up and saw a woman standing before her with long blond hair and a calm look on her fine featured face. She was a beautiful woman. Gabby knew immediately this must be her mother's friend, Mo Mo Kelly. She stood lowering her hand to call Jack to her side.

'Sssh! old man, I think we're amongst friends here.'

'Gabriella, thank God you've made it. I've been worried sick,' she said, smiling putting out her hand, 'I'm Mo Mo.'

Gabby shook her hand and introduced Jack who promptly licked her hand.

'Traitor,' Gabby said with a smile.

'Come on you two, you must be famished' she said walking ahead out of the clearing and onto a trail through the exotic trees, bushes and plants.

Gabby was astounded by the sounds of birds chirping, the butterflies lazily passing them by, the subtle noises made by the breeze through the branches and leaves.

As they reached another smaller clearing amongst the towering evergreens, Mo Mo stopped and turned to Gabby.

'Before I forget there's something I must ask of you, Gabriella.'

Gabby stared at her and answered smiling,

'Yes?'

'I must see the mark. I'm sure you are who I think you are, but we'd better make sure huh?'

'Absolutely, if you tell me what mark you're talking about,' Gabby replied watching her for any kind of reaction.

Mo Mo moved forward and touched the back of her own neck.

'You have a birthmark of a feather located below your hairline, about here, if I remember correctly.'

Now Gabby was surprised, not by the knowledge of the birthmark but the fact she'd seen it.

'I er, you know me?' she asked in amazement.

'Of course, I know you, darling. We met when you were very, very young. You were the one who gave me my name, because you found Mo Mo much easier to say than Maureen.'

Gabby was stunned but the more she thought about her early childhood the more she remembered a fun-loving girlfriend of her mother's. Gabby leaned down letting her long hair fall forward exposing the nape of her neck. There, highly visible on her light olive skin was a beautifully detailed pale white feather, about an inch and a half long. Mo Mo bent down and gently touched it before taking Gabby's hand and helping her back to her feet.

On they walked for another twenty minutes, Gabby having to stop here and there to watch the array of exotic birds that followed them.

'What a magical place this is,' she said to her hostess after a flock of red billed parakeets flew by screaming like a bunch of unruly school children.

'It is indeed,' Mo Mo said, as they entered a large clearing. Mo Mo pointed to the far side saying,

'Ah, here we are, my home.'

Gabby blinked a couple of times, focusing on the rather drab little cottage in the distance. Such beauty all around and now this plain little house, she was dumbfounded.

'It's so, er pretty,' was all she could stutter.

'Come, my dear, wait until you see the inside,' Mo Mo said smiling and holding her hand once more.

I'm so excited,' Gabby said to Jack, 'Aren't you?'

Jack bounded ahead, happy to be in anything with a roof. Upon nearing Mo Mo's home Gabby stopped and looked up, she saw no roof, just lush tree branches draping down where the roof should be. Now her interest was piqued.

Mo Mo opened the door and in they traipsed. The ground floor was one big room with a huge fireplace at one end. At the other end was a functioning kitchen. There were big stuffed couches and thick woollen throw rugs everywhere, but no beds, no TV, no bathrooms, nothing.

'Bet your hungry, yes?' Mo Mo asked turning on the electric kettle.

It took Gabby a few seconds to realize there was electricity, so far from the mainland. She knew all about petrol driven generators and gas powered ovens from years of camping, but the more her eyes roamed the house the more she was convinced Mo Mo was plugged into the mains supply.

Mo Mo made some ham sandwiches for Gabby and Jack which were wolfed down by both with equal enthusiasm. After all hunger was sated, Gabby sipped her hot tea and scrutinized her mother's friend.

'Could you tell me a little about yourself, or am I being a bit rude?' Gabby asked.

As Jack had passed out on the floor making all kinds of unnatural noises, the women decided to sit on a couch beside the fire.

'No darling, you're not being rude' said Mo Mo reassuringly touching Gabby's hand. She rubbed her chin with elegant fingers, obviously contemplating where exactly to start.

'Your mother and I became friends when we both turned fifteen and realised our birthdays were on the same day. We became much closer a year or so later after what happened in France,' she said softly, not sure if Gabby knew the whole story.

'When my mother was raped and I was conceived you mean,' said Gabby matter-of-factly.

'Yes. You understand, of course, that, being a traveller, things were tough at school. The other students were cruel people, convinced they were better than the gypsies. Your mother, Caitlan, was both smart and strong-willed and I instantly took to her and the great positive image she had of herself.'

'It was as if Caitlan constantly reinvented Caitlan every week. It was quite magical to watch her. Anyway, after the rape and all the anger from her parents that went with it, your mother would come and stay with me and my Ma in Letterfrack. My mother is still a vet there. The initial anger on your grandparents' side was directed fully toward the family of the rapist, not toward your mother.'

Mo Mo paused for a minute while topping up their teacups.

'So anyway, as time went by, and you began to grow inside your mother, she was taken out of school. It was around six months after you were conceived that your grandfather disappeared for several weeks. It wasn't until recently that I heard where he'd gone. He had found your father, a Romany gypsy named Malut Menjanii and his brother, in a brothel in Tangiers.'

'He first slit the throat of the brother before tying up and castrating your father leaving him to bleed out. It was a brutal attack and one he's never been prosecuted for.'

Gabby was stunned and quite shaken by all this news. She rose and warmed her hands behind her by the fire. After a few seconds she yawned and stretched, looking at Mo Mo and Jack who continued to snore on the floor.

The women were both contemplating the seriousness of Gabby's grandfather's actions when suddenly Jack let out a long and soon very odorous sound. The women burst out in simultaneous laughter startling the old dog to his feet.

After wiping away the tears of merriment, Mo Mo stood and motioned Gabby to follow.

'Let me show you to your room.'

Gabby was slightly puzzled by this considering they

were in the only room she could see. Mo Mo opened a door hidden in the back wall of the cottage. Once through, they ascended some stairs. Upon reaching the top Gabby was completely awe-struck. It was certainly a magical place.

She walked around and around the big bedroom staring through the glass ceiling at the canopy of trees above. They were lush and tropical in nature with every kind of exotic bird flying around or perched on branches grooming themselves.

She spotted many different types of parakeets, macaws, hummingbirds and even the one from the old Guinness commercials.

'What's the one with the long beak? Oh, I can't remember,' she asked Mo Mo laughing.

'Toucans,' said Mo Mo, obviously pleased by the young woman's joy.

Gabby ran back out of the house, Jack following behind, excited by whatever was going on. She stared long and hard at the canopy above the cottage but could see nothing out of the ordinary. It was only after she leaned against a tree that answers began to reveal themselves. She rapped her knuckles on the 'tree' and it echoed back.

It seemed to Gabby like some kind of thick bamboo of sorts but obviously wasn't. She searched the clearing with her eyes highly focused and spotted several more of the same kind. Mo Mo came up beside her smiling.

'Did you work it out yet?' she asked. Gabby also noticed what appeared to be millions of tiny glass beads above the canopy.

'Is there some kind of tent above the house?' Gabby inquired.

'Indeed there is. Come on, I'll show you.'

She led her back up stairs. Another hidden door led from the bedroom they'd been in, down a hallway past several more rooms and ended in a large living/sitting room.

Mo Mo pressed a button beside the light switch and the

glass roof slowly slid back revealing the chatter and noise from the birds above. A large white cockatoo glided down, landing on Mo Mo's shoulder.

'Perdita, my love, how are we today?' she asked the bird.

'I'm grand, mama, sure the grass is wet,' replied the cockatoo.

Gabby stared absolutely dumbfounded at the conversation taking place.

'What does she mean the grass is wet?' Gabby asked.

'That means er, like nothing has changed, all is well in the world. Ah sure the grass is wet . . . means all okay. You understand?' Mo Mo asked.

Gabby half nodded and half shook her head as if getting it but not all of it,

'Yes, I think so,' was all she could reply.

There was a carved wooden spiral staircase in one corner which they ascended. Up on the roof under the trees there was a huge wooden deck with views out over the ocean beyond. Mo Mo led Gabby to the edge of the canopy of trees and showed her the secret of the roof.

Gabby felt the mesh-like substance.

'What is it?' she asked.

'My late husband, Peter, was a pioneer in the use of solar technology amongst many other things. Anyway, he developed these microscopic photovoltaic solar cells that he then weaved with thousands of miles of gossamer thread to form this membrane,' Mo Mo said proudly.

'He weaved all this himself?' asked Gabby wide-eyed.

Mo Mo laughed and replied,

'Oh, no. In his travels he met a man in China with a huge weaving mill. They specialised in silks and the finest of threads, and so he asked him if he'd be interested and the man said yes.'

Mo Mo pointed along the edges of the canopy showing Gabby how it was all stretched and held together, anchoring itself to the camouflaged steel girders erected in the ground below.

Gabby stepped up onto a chair looking above the membrane and saw that the trees and plants weren't nearly as lush as they seemed from below. They looked like average trees from above.

'You see, Peter never quite envisioned the heat that would be generated by this system, hence the very tropical foliage,' Mo Mo said proudly.

'And you get electricity from this?'

'More than enough to run five or six houses the size of this one.'

'Wow! Why all the secrecy? The hidden doors, the hidden house, the inaccessibility of the island?'

'My late husband was a very secretive man. I realize now I hardly knew him at all,' she said softly, her voice cracking with emotion.

'You loved him very much, no?' Gabby asked.

'Oh yes. We met when I was eighteen and he was fifty three. He swept me off my feet with his acerbic wit and rakish good looks.'

'Sounds lovely but where did his money come from to do all this?' she asked.

Mo Mo thought for awhile before replying.

'I have no idea.' All I know is he protected this place, this Shangri La, with the ferocity of a wolf protecting its cubs.'

'Huh, I wish I'd met him. I think he and I would have got on,' Gabby said stepping back down onto the wooden decking.

'I think you probably would,' Mo Mo said, holding Gabby's hand, leading her back down the hall.

'You have a choice of these two bedrooms,' she said pointing to the doors. 'Each with their own baths.'

Gabby took the one with a porthole window to the sea. She jumped up on the bed and sunk into the fluffy pillows and goose down comforter. After lying there for several seconds she yawned and said,

'I'm exhausted, do you mind if I have a little nap?'

'Not at all. I'll show Jack around. Sleep as long as you like,' Mo Mo said smiling, as she lead the reluctant Jack down the stairs, pulling the door half closed behind her.

CHAPTER 17

Jane slowed upon reaching the garda station. She'd driven like a banshee on acid, tearing through the woods and trees with little regard for her safety. Henry had decided early on that flying alongside was far safer than being perched on her shoulder.

She pulled into the parking lot of the police station, did a 360 degree turn on the quad bike, checking no one had followed her. Nobody had.

Garda Shanahan had had a tough few days since the attack at the campsite. His girlfriend, or so he'd hoped, Sheila, had promptly disappeared; the special weapons person had done the same. He'd been demoted to a desk job pending further inquiry and even the Garda bloodhound had vanished into thin air. So when the door to the station burst open and in flew a screeching parrot of some kind and a screaming woman, covered head to toe in mud, he felt he'd totally lost his mind.

'Yee ha! Howdy Sheriff, der be a murder in these them parts!' screeched Henry, still high from the great escape.

'Madam, did you see the sign?' he said officiously pointing to the placard on the wall. It says no animals except seeing eye dogs.

Jane glanced at the sign, ignored it and marched up to the counter.

'You stupid man! This bird is my witness!'

Shanahan leaned forward wrinkling his nose at the pungent odour emanating from the woman.

'Witness to what exactly, Madam?'

'I killed someone. They were trying to kill me. Would you please come and see for yourself?' Jane said, calming down for a moment.

Shanahan pondered the news for a few seconds before making a decision. He pulled down the shutter deciding it was close enough to lunchtime to do so. Ushering the bird and woman out the door, he locked up the station, moving quickly to his patrol car.

'Where to?' he asked, opening the passenger door.

'Letterfrack. Can we bring my bird?' she asked.

Shanahan took one look at the bedraggled creature and nodded in the affirmative. Shanahan's only motive in doing this was to get out from behind the desk and, hopefully, solve a crime, thus reinstating himself as a top investigator once more.

Half way to Letterfrack and the vet's house, Mark Shanahan was ready to kill Henry, the cockatoo. So far on the journey, the bird had nearly caused several accidents with its ear splitting screeches crying 'Watch out!'and its directions: 'Take a left! or take a right!'

He stopped the car and turned to Jane.

'Can you not keep your bird under control? Please!' he implored.

'Can't do!' Henry replied.

The garda got out, asking her to join him on the roadside.

'We have two alternatives here,' he said assertively. 'One, I go on alone or two, it,' pointing to the bird, 'surely can fly alongside the car.'

Jane opened the passenger door.

'Henry, out!'

The cockatoo pulled one wing up in front of its face and uttered in a pitiful childlike voice,

'Me?'

Jane stood, expressionless, hands on hips.

'Out!'

Henry waddled across the seats like a penguin and flew out the door, landing on the Garda car's light bar.

'Yee Ha. Let's get them varmints,' he shrilled.

Even Jane and Mark had to laugh at the bird's antics.

'Where did he learn all this?'

'We think they were in a circus or travelling show when younger. Henry and his sister were unwanted and so I volunteered to take them. My daughter has the sister.'

'How old is he?'

'Well, they live up to ninety years and so your guess is probably as good as mine.'

Jane gave the policeman directions to the back path she had barrelled down only one hour earlier. They parked a couple of hundred yards away from the main building only because Henry was still perched on the light bar making siren sounds.

'You two stay here and you . . . ' pointing to the bird, 'no noise, please,' Mark said.

'No prob man,' was Henry's reply. 'All you had to do was be nice you know.'

The vet and the Garda smiled at this as he removed his handgun from the boot of the car.

'Listen Jane,' he said, cocking his weapon, 'if you hear gunshots or I'm not back within fifteen minutes, take my car and wait in Letterfrack for other Gardaí. They should be here within the hour, okay?' he said pulling the Velcro straps tight on the bulletproof vest.

'Okay,' she said nodding, as he strode off down the path.

After ten minutes, Jane started pacing beside the car and then Henry, to add to her concern, started to go 'Tick

Tock Tick Tock,' repeatedly.

Garda Shanahan had approached the house with extreme caution, remembering all his skills from the days at the police academy. The vet had given him the make and model of her own car and he was pleased to see it parked where she'd said it would be. The other vehicle she had described was nowhere to be seen. He entered the rear of the house, pausing every few seconds, listening for any kind of sounds. There were none.

He was back at the squad car within fifteen minutes much to Jane's relief.

'No sign of anyone, dead or alive,' he said.

'Tell me again about the one you disposed of.'

'Er, mid thirties, I'd say, long, black hair, five foot eight roughly, brown eyes, I think,' Jane said studying his face, 'You know her don't you?'

'I fear I might. It sounds like my Garda partner, Sheila Russell, but I don't understand. She was working with me for the past year or so.'

'Maybe she was a plant. Keeping her eyes open for something or someone.'

'I suppose it's possible but I'd feel better if you had somewhere else to go for a couple of days, least until we catch the Frenchman.'

Jane glanced at Henry for a second and made up her mind.

'I know a place no one will find me. Is it okay to take my car?' she asked.

Shanahan hesitated briefly before replying,

'I'm sure it will be fine. Let's just go and check it out first.'

After making sure the car was untouched he let her and Henry leave the area, deciding he'd be in enough trouble, when the bosses got there. She'd be better off avoiding the rigorous cross examination that was sure to follow.

CHAPTER 18

Philippe knew there were no members of the Irish police force located in Cleggan. So he reasoned the vet would have reported the holdup to the station in Clifden, thus no immediate connection to him or his whereabouts.

Donning his disguise once more, he wandered seemingly aimlessly from one to another of the four bars in Cleggan, listening for anything unusual in the area in the last day or two.

In the Pier Bar he picked up the story of someone called Crabapple Jones having a boat stolen by a girl and her dog. Rather than ask the old fisherman for directions to the Jones's house, he paid for his pint and left. The old man consistently pointed south along the beach while telling his tale and so Philippe took the same direction.

CJ had the boat upside down on blocks, still cursing the girl for the damage she'd caused him. In all honesty though, he was more worried than anything. The girl and dog were nowhere to be seen when he'd reached his sinking boat.

He'd mentioned it to a few of the locals he could trust to keep a lookout for them, but hadn't reported the incident to the police for fear he'd actually seen what he thought he'd seen: a flying girl. They'd probably lock him up in a rubber room and throw away the key.

He was replacing the transom and part of the stern when he heard footsteps on the stones behind him. He turned slowly holding a hammer in his hand.

'Whoaa!' said Philippe, raising his hands in mock surrender. 'I mean no harm to you,' he added exaggerating his French accent.

CJ, remembering the hammer, dropped it to his side.

'I'm sorry I wasn't thinking.'

'It's okay, you seem a little, er, how you say, detracted non?'

'I think you mean distracted. Indeed, I am a little,' he replied, looking the Frenchman up and down. The Irish are somewhat wary of strangers, especially in small rural villages like Cleggan. Crabapple Jones was no exception.

'I was wondering if you can help me?' Philippe asked.

Jones turned back to the boat and continued working.

'I will if I can.'

Philippe walked alongside staring at the damaged vessel.

'You had an accident?' he inquired cautiously.

The young man eyed him carefully before replying.

'I did. But that's not what you wanted to know, right?'

The veteran killer pretended shock at the abruptness of the boy.

'Mais oui, I'm sorry, I am searching for my niece. I heard you might have seen her.'

CJ stopped work and stood up to his full height, hammer definitely brandished this time.

'I have no idea what you're talking about mister, you must be mistaken.' Philippe pulled out a crumpled photograph taken from afar of an unaware Gabriella.

'Please, I hear the men in the bar talking. She's my only relative, I am very worried,' he said thrusting the photo forward.

Gabriella, Jones thought to himself glancing at the

picture without recognition. *What a beautiful name for such a beautiful girl.* But she had been both scared and anxious when stealing his boat. Maybe this person was one of the reasons why.

'Ah yes,' said Jones, 'She had a dog with her. I remember now.' he added.

Philippe replaced the photograph in his jacket pocket, thrilled the boy had seen her.

'Yes yes, a dog with her, please, where did she go?'

Jones scratched his head before replying.

'What is the name of her dog? You must know if you are who you say you are,' he said, tossing the hammer between his hands.

Philippe stood back, watching the young man carefully.

'It's Jasper, that's his name.'

Jones had clearly heard the girl shouting for Jack to get into his boat. Nobody would change the name of their dog so late in its life, so this man was no uncle of Gabriella's.

'Indeed it is,' said Jones, smiling. He looked across the bay before pointing to a white cottage opposite from where they stood.

'She wanted to borrow my boat to visit her sick aunt who lives over there.'

'And, you lend to her?' asked the Frenchman expectantly.

'Hell no, I need my boat,' Jones said turning back toward the village. 'But you should know the aunt and where she lives?'

Let's see how you get out of this one, he thought to himself.

Philippe studied the young man briefly but intently.

'So you give her the boat? Where did she go?' he continued.

Pointing to the secondary road on the other side of the village, CJ said,

'I told her to take the Renvyle bus to Derryinver. From there she could walk to the aunt's home'.

'And she left then?' Philippe asked as if relieved.

'Yep, off she went.'

Philippe thanked the young man and walked back down the beach toward Cleggan once more, knowing Jones was sending him on a fool's errand. He would watch carefully for the boy's next move, sure in the fact he had some knowledge of Gabriella's whereabouts.

CHAPTER 19

Gabriella slept the sleep of a thousand nights. She woke to the tropical sounds from the trees above. At first she didn't remember where she was. But then, as she wiped the sleep from her eyes, all her memories flooded back. She was safe and alive. *What more could anyone want*, she thought to herself.

As soon as she stirred, Jack, all freshly washed and fed, leapt up onto the bed and took it upon himself to try to lick her to the point of suffocation or maybe drowning.

Glancing up at the ceiling, she noticed the roof had been partially retracted and sitting on the ledge above the bedroom wall was the white cockatoo, Perdita, or was it a parakeet? She couldn't remember. She was still half awake when another bird of similar design landed beside the first.

She sat up and rubbed her eyes again. Was she seeing double? The next thing that happened startled her.

'Up and at 'em!' screeched the newcomer.

'Shut up!' replied Perdita.

Thankfully for Gabby, Mo Mo came into the room and closed the glass roof over, silencing the birds on the trees.

'Am I seeing two birds or one?' she asked.

Mo Mo smiled, 'Two. Henry belongs to my mother.

She sent him ahead to let me know she's coming. They're very clever birds.'

'Huh,' was all Gabby could think of saying while watching them dip and soar, chasing one another around and around.

'I was afraid to wake you,' she said sitting on the end of the bed holding out a glass of water. Gabby took the glass, took a big gulp and said smiling,

'Let the birds do it instead?'

'One can never be too careful with sleepy teenagers.'

She walked to the closet, revealing shelves and hangers full of girls' clothes.

'These are for you,' Mo Mo said, proudly.

Gabby stood, concealing herself with a sheet.

'How? When? Wow!' she said laughing and touching the shirts and pants and dresses.

Mo Mo's eyes lit up upon seeing the young woman's happiness.

'Your mother called me a few weeks ago and said there was a strong possibility that you might visit soon and so I went shopping.'

The joy of the moment disappeared as quickly as it had come. Gabby went back and sat on the edge of the bed head bowed, tears trickling down her cheeks. Mo Mo rushed to her side placing her arm around her shoulders.

'I'm sorry, darling. I didn't think. How stupid of me,' she said.

Gabby lifted the other woman's hand, placing it on her lap. She raised her head and smiled softly.

'Please don't worry. It's just the way it is and something I will have to get used to. Thank you for taking care of me.'

She lifted Mo Mo's hand to her mouth and kissed it gently.

They sat there for a few moments, heads touching, until Mo Mo said,

'Why don't you take a shower or a bath and come meet

me downstairs when you're ready? I'll have some food prepared.'

Gabby went into the bathroom quietly closing the door behind her.

CHAPTER 20

Scafa had made it clear to her clan that she wanted to travel alone. No followers on this trip she'd said. This was personal. There was one exception to the rule of course. Visnik had travelled with her on the boat and train but not anywhere close to her. They hadn't acknowledged each other at any stage of the journey.

Scafa wore an old Connemara-style black woollen shawl and spoke to nobody, giving the impression of someone in grief, suffering the loss of one recently departed. She laughed to herself that the departed one had not yet departed, but if she had anything to do with it, the girl would be well on her way soon.

Visnik had other ideas. His sole interest in this enterprise was keeping the girl alive for his experimentations. From the sparse information he had gleaned from Scafa, the girl had unnatural powers. His plan would be to keep her secured in the dungeons below his castle and somehow release those powers for his own advantage. His followers believed there should be a picture of him in the dictionary beside the word narcissist because he worshipped the ground he walked on.

They arrived in Galway and booked into adjoining rooms in a run-down hotel behind the train station.

That night lying in each other's arms for the first time in forty years, they hatched their plans for the fate of Gabriella O'Toole. Visnik had received word from his number one assassin, Philippe, that the trail had gone cold somewhere around a place called Cleggan on the Atlantic coast.

They both agreed separation in the morning would be the prudent thing to do, so they slept.

Garda Mark Shanahan was back at the desk in the Clifden Police station while his bosses reviewed his conduct over the past few days. He was very disturbed by the vet's story, the shootings, the disappearing body of his missing partner. He was so confused and preoccupied doing a Sudoku puzzle that he didn't even hear the door open.

It was only when a gnarled old hand crept across the counter that he came out of his funk. It looked like something out of a horror movie. He gasped at the knobby knuckles, the thin blue veins ready to pop from the parchment like skin. He lifted his eyes to the face and gasped even louder as the ancient woman opened her mouth to speak.

The teeth were broken and black; the lips had recoiled to resemble squashed slugs. The face was like well-cured haddock and the eyes, the eyes he'd never seen anything like them before. The pupils were like liquid silver floating on miniscule pools of blood.

'Jaysus! What the . . . ?' he said, sliding back the glass security partition he'd moved to open the paper and complete the game of Sudoku.

After closing it, he suddenly remembered her wizened old hand. Thankfully she'd removed it before he'd accidently sliced it off.

'Please relax young man. I merely need some questions answered and then I will be on my way. Is this okay with you?' she asked fixing him with a stare that could freeze the oceans.

Mark was unable to utter a word. He was transfixed by her stare and scared by her looks. He merely nodded like a guilty child about to be admonished.

'First of all, I am from Poland, a small village outside Warsaw. My family are all dead, from wars, communism, illness, but mainly dead from feud, you know this word?' she asked the Garda.

'Yes, I know that word,' Mark said, finally finding his tongue.

'Good, well not good, really,' said Scafa with a haunting chest-rattling cackle.

Shanahan thought for a second she might keel over - hoped it actually- but it was not to be.

'I search for my stupid grandson. He is the only part of family I have left. I think he might have got mixed up in feud over here against gypsies called O'Toole. This you have heard of?'

Garda Shanahan became suddenly alert. The only dead bodies they'd found were from the family of O'Tooles. Unless she meant the Frenchman. Maybe he'd gone missing since the incident at the vet's house.

Couldn't blame him really if this one was his boss, he thought.

'In order to release any information I might have, I'll need to see your passport please,' said the Garda nervously.

Scafa rolled her eyes, lifted a big leather handbag from her feet and plonked it on the counter.

'This is really necessary? I am just an old woman seeking out my grandson,' she said opening the clasp and rummaging in the bag.

Mark noticed the gold arm bracelet on her wrist and commented,

'That's a fine piece of work, may I ask where you got it? The detail is superb, I'd guess Romania or maybe Hungary no?'

'No!' she said scowling.

She closed her bag, hung it on her right arm and looked him in the eyes.

'No, I am sorry, I must leave passport in car. One minute please.'

She pulled her shawl around her shoulders and walked out of the door.

Shanahan took a couple of seconds too long. By the time he'd made it from the counter to the door the fragile old woman was nowhere to be seen. He stood in the car park scratching his head, unable to comprehend how she could have vanished so quickly.

Visnik had been listening to the whole conversation in the police station. As soon as he heard the prearranged signal of the handbag's clasp clicking shut, he picked the lock on the rear fire exit door.

Shanahan moved back behind the counter, still confused by her disappearance and ultimately unaware of the blinking light on the security console notifying the presence of an intruder.

One of features of modern architecture is that, although beautiful in design, it often disguises nooks and crannies in which anyone with an ounce of ingenuity could find a suitable hiding place. The porch on the police station jutted out two feet from the main building with one of the many cast-iron drainpipes running vertically alongside. With her light and wiry frame, Scafa had merely grasped the holding brackets and climbed above the front door.

Before the Garda could call for backup, he felt cold steel pressed against the back of his neck. Visnik pulled him back into the main office, away from the counter. Scafa returned, locking the front door behind her.

Visnik held him tight as Scafa approached, raising her right index finger to her slug lips.

'Ssshh,' she said before uncovering her left arm. The gold bracelet shone in the neon lights above.

'Now, Mr Policeman, we are needing some information from you and you will tell us all that we seek, yes?' she said.

Shanahan tried to struggle but was no match for the superior strength of Visnik.

'Here we are. Pay attention please,' she said pointing her left index finger at the coffee pot below the window.

She flexed it down and up again quickly. There was a subtle *ppphut* as one of the microscopic compressed gas canisters above her wrist released an unpoisoned dart, causing the glass of the pot to explode into tiny fragments.

'Impressed?' Visnik asked.

'Not particularly. Who are you people and what's with the hag's eyes?' said Shanahan calmly.

'Bind him to the chair!' screamed Scafa, spittle flying from her mouth.

'Palms up!' she added.

'I show you to be scared of me!' she said moving above his clamped arm.

'What, you're going to undress? Now that would scare me,' said Shanahan grinning.

Scafa, furious by now, made a fist just above the garda's ulnar artery that runs from the arm to the hand. She shot a dart right through the vein causing some serious pain but more dangerous than that was the fine fountain of blood gushing from it.

Then she moved to the other hand and threatened the same thing.

'You know, I can do this all day in all sorts of places until finally you will bleed out?' she said grinning.

'Give it your best shot,' said Mark, not quite as confidently as before.

'Oh I will, believe me,' she said moving to his other wrist.

'Where is the girl?' she asked.

'What girl?' he replied as she shot into the other vein.

'Jaysus! Go easy! I don't know what you're talking

about, I swear.'

Visnik leaned over him.

'What about the Frenchman and his woman? Any ideas about them?' he whispered into Shanahan's ear.

Scafa saw the scared look in the garda's face and instantly knew the man had some information they needed.

'Take off his pants!' she ordered.

'Okay, okay okay.'

He knew he wasn't a hero and so he told them everything he knew about Jane, the vet, disappearing to some safe haven. He told them what he knew about the assassins but said he didn't know where they were. He swore to himself that if he lived he would get his revenge.

They left him there bound and gagged with two holes in his wrists, sure that he wouldn't last the hour.

CHAPTER 21

The message handed to Crabapple Jones was a series of numbers based on an old World War II code. Simply put, if the sender wanted the first letter to be A they would write 2, second letter an L they would write the number 9. Although the letter L was number twelve in the alphabet the code number was 9. It was a progressive subtraction method. Whatever the next number was, he would subtract 4 and so on.

That night he read the note from Kelly's Island. It was supplied by the Cleggan Marine Radio Service, used primarily for ships seeking a variety of amenities in the area and local fishermen needing weather updates. Mobile and Internet communications were unreliable on the island. Both services were spotty at best.

The message read:

CJ, please wait for Jane. Be more cautious than usual. Dangerous people seeking guest. Be safe. MM.

As he tore up the note and scattered it into the fire he pondered its meaning. The first thing that struck him was 'the guest'. Apart from Mrs Kelly's mother, Jane, he couldn't recall any guests to the island.

'Stranger and stranger,' he said to himself, thinking first

about the girl who had stolen his boat and then the nosey little Frenchman earlier that day. He was pretty sure one thing had something to do with the other, but what?

Before turning in he phoned his friend Marshy and told him what he needed him to do. He then made one other call to Jane.

At five o'clock the next morning just as the first light of dawn crept slowly over the hills off to the east of Connemara, the young man left the Jones house, carrying a box full of what, to Philippe, looked like food supplies. He walked down to the shore placing the items into his recently restored boat. He then returned to the house and repeated the exercise several more times until the boat was packed full.

The previous night, Philippe had received a phone call from friends in Marseilles recommending a part time drug runner and smuggler from Galway as one who could assist him in his mission. The man's name was Stinky McBride and this morning he was awaiting instructions from the Frenchman.

'I hope you're ready?' asked Philippe into his phone.

'Start the engine, please, and standby,' was all he said, not bothering to wait for a reply.

As soon as young Jones set off, the assassin would call for his ride. He'd told Stinky to bring some extra hardware as the shotguns he'd stolen from the vet were a bit conspicuous when walking in daylight around populated areas.

'Jaysus, Mrs Stephens, does he ever stop talking?' asked Crabapple, referring to Henry, of course, who'd flown back to hurry things along. Jane smiled as she lifted a crate of tins onto her shoulder.

'Now CJ, don't you know by now the answer to that?'

She walked steadily down the gangplank of the *Dopey Runt* as Marshy had christened her when he had bought her, aged fourteen. He now had three lobster boats at the ripe old age of twenty. They were all moored in

Derryinver.

He and Jonesy, as he liked to call his friend, had swapped places at three that morning. The previous night had been blacker than black itself and if anyone was watching they'd have seen nothing untoward. Jones had warned his friend to be on the lookout for a balding little 'Frenchie' and if danger loomed to ditch the plan and save himself.

Marshy had scoffed at that idea saying he was well able to look after himself. The main reason for the swap was Jane didn't know Marshy and CJ felt it better if he met her given all that she'd been through.

An hour later as the young man cast off from the beach, the Frenchman nodded his head approvingly.

'He has timed it well,' Philippe said to himself referring to the rising tide.

He pressed the call back number.

'You may come now and pick me up,' he said, hanging up immediately.

Stinky McBride scratched his ass, farted, readjusted his privates, hacked up a loogey and spat it into the boat he was tied up beside in Cleggan harbour. He cast off the bow and stern lines, lit a cigarette, started the engines and puttered out into the bay. His boat was a rusty old deep water trawler called *Black Mindy* named after the only woman he'd ever loved.

He heaved to off the rocks west of Cleggan, lowered the punt and picked up the assassin.

'What's with the name?' asked Jane as they too left the safety of the shores.

'*Dopey Runt* was what Marshy's father had called him growing up and it wasn't a term of affection,' said Jones steering out into the northern part of Ballinakill Bay. Cleggan and Marshy were roughly ten miles to the south.

Reaching the edges of the bay, Marshy turned slowly eyeing the large trawler barely moving five hundred yards behind. He and Jones had discussed this the previous night and decided there was no need to rush things. Besides, *The Dopey Runt* needed time to reach the rendezvous point.

Stinky Mc Bride didn't like to run his engines so slowly and was getting impatient with the speed of the loaded currach ahead.

'Can't I just run him over and be done with it?' he asked.

Philippe nearing the end of his patience stuck a gun in the big man's back,

'No! you're being paid enough, just back off!'

McBride didn't appreciate the gun in his kidneys and wouldn't forget it anytime soon.

Four hours later the *Dopey Runt* reached the west side of the island known as Morag's Revenge, an unforgiving chunk of basalt and limestone twenty miles from Kelly's Island.

Jones had moored the boat a hundred yards from the rocky shoreline and was lowering a dinghy. Jane held the line while he climbed in.

'Is this a good idea?' she asked, eyeing this unwelcome place.

'Tis fine, Mrs Stephens. Sure, haven't Marshy and me been here a million times before.'

'Let the rope go, please. I'll be back in no time,' he said starting up the little outboard motor, pointing for the beach.

Once there, he tied the painter to a sharp black outcrop and scooted up the easily climbed rockface.

Now in open water, Marshy was having little problem controlling the boat, mainly because most of the cases and crates lashed on board were, in fact, empty. He knew he was reaching the point where his pursuers' reaction to seeing Morag's Revenge might make them get a bit silly and attack the boat, thinking they had found the island where the girl was hiding. He was ready in case that happened.

He was right. Half a mile from the island's eastern

shore he heard the revving up of diesel engines and, upon looking back, he saw a small bald man cradling a machine gun standing on the bow bracing his leg on the gunwale aiming right at him.

Marshy flicked the throttle on the outboard and spun the tiller hard to port causing the skeg to dramatically change the direction of the currach. Bullets zinged by his head, peppering the side of the boat.

'Bollocks to this,' he screamed, diving off the side and into the cold Atlantic water. The bullets were popping around him, so he submerged, striking out for shore.

Crabapple was watching all this from atop the rocky cliffs. He was no sniper but he did know which end of the gun to point. He'd taken it from Marshy's lobster boat just in case something went wrong and something was definitely going wrong. As he sighted down the rusty old Remington rifle, two things came to mind.

One, if it was as rusty and corroded on the inside he could be in trouble and second, why did Marshy have it in the first place. Giant lobsters?

The big trawler was bearing down on his little boat. Once he'd seen his friend jump overboard he'd released the safety. He squeezed the trigger gently, closing his eyes in fear the gun might blow up, knowing if that was the case it wouldn't really help much.

The bullet left the chamber and struck the wheelhouse, causing a small star to form in the glass. Sadly, it didn't slow McBride down. In fact, it made him so furious he careened into the smaller boat sinking it instantly.

Philippe was unprepared for the impact and so fell forward, his head barely missing the gunwale. Groggy still, he looked down at the wreckage. It wasn't the splintered boat that caught his attention as much as the floating boxes all around. He lifted the boat hook and snagged one of them. It was empty.

Turning to McBride he screamed,

'It's a trap, reverse engines!' Then he noticed the starry

patterns appearing regularly in the glass.

'What the . . .?' Philippe said focusing on the cliffs and seeing nothing and then scanning the breaking surf, seeing no sign of the boy but something else looming from below.

Rocks! Stop!'

His warning, even if heard, would've probably been ignored. McBride was livid.

As Marshy scrambled onto the rocky beach, *Black Mindy* struck a reef. The cutting-edged rocks sliced a four foot hole in the steel plated trawler stopping it in its tracks. The Frenchman was staring at the island. Before he could retrieve his Uzi submachine gun, Marshy was up and over the ridge line.

'Look what you did, ya dirty little shite! You'll be paying for this!' McBride said storming out of the wheelhouse.

Philippe calmly glanced at the large man approaching him, clicked off the safety, made sure it was back on single shot and put a bullet through Stinky's forehead. The big man crumpled to the deck.

Philippe had always taken his job seriously and so he lowered the life raft into the choppy swell. After dropping in the gun and some spare clips of ammunition, he climbed aboard the inflatable and began rowing toward the shore. Alas his luck, like everything else, deserted him also. The inflatable deflated and started to sink. He barely made it the little island.

On the far side, the lads were slipping and sliding down the shale slope above the beach, laughing and jabbering about the close call they'd just had. It was all an adventure to them.

Once aboard the lobster boat, Jones took the precaution of heading due east in case the Frenchman was watching them.

The Frenchman was watching them, but was unable to do anything to stop them. He'd been taken for a ride and now his ride was sinking. He threw the gun on the ground in frustration knowing this failure would probably cost him his life. Visnik was about as forgiving as Attila the Hun. His only option, he felt, was to disappear.

He sat on a rock overlooking the flailing trawler. *It would sink soon*, he thought to himself. His reputation as a top killer was gone, hoodwinked by two kids, his Sheila was gone. There was really nothing else for it.

He stood above the rocks, put the gun under his chin and fired, his body falling into the ocean below.

CHAPTER 22

After eating, Gabby and Jack went exploring the island. The magnificent colours of the tropical foliage could only lift her spirits. She was beginning to feel this could be the place for understanding both her future and her powers. Once outside the canopy though, she felt the real world encroaching once more and the reality that she was a hunted girl. She wondered what was to become of her.

Mo Mo beckoned her over and they walked along the cliff edge for a few minutes until she stopped, pointing to the red and white little fishing boat seemingly sailing right into harm's way.

'What are . . . ?' she stopped herself, remembering the directions for landing on the island, by boat. She hadn't needed those directions. Gabby could see three people on the deck waving up at them, Mo Mo returning the greeting.

However, Gabby was not so thrilled at the sight of the new arrivals. She was uncomfortable not knowing who they were and what their agendas were. That's what comes from living on the edge from such a young age.

Mo Mo took Gabby's hand, sensing the girl's reluctance. They walked slowly down to the hidden bay which the boat would soon enter.

'It's okay Gabby. It's just my mother and the young man who supplies me with necessities every week,' she said softly.

'So who's the other man?' Gabby asked, suspiciously.

'Probably just a friend. Believe me, you're in no danger here,' she replied.

Gabby sighed and smiled at Mo Mo as the lobster boat emerged from the natural stone archway and into the little bay.

'I'm sorry, I'm still just a bit scared,' she said glancing over to the people on the deck.

'Oh crap!' she exclaimed putting her hand to her mouth both in embarrassment and shock. There was one person on the boat who wasn't smiling at all. Crabapple Jones!

Mo Mo stared at Gabby, then at Jones and could see some definite friction between them as he tied up at the wharf.

'What's wrong?'

Gabby didn't know whether to run or fly or extend her talons.

'Er, nothing really. I, er, just stole and wrecked his boat,' she said, pointing to the young man she'd tricked a day and a half earlier.

'Oh, don't worry about that. It was probably my boat anyway. CJ won't mind,' said Mo Mo, marching down to hug her mother.

Before Gabby could explain, Henry and Perdita came flying out of the trees shrieking like a couple of schoolgirls.

The two men stepped off the boat. Jones approached Gabby as Marshy began unloading.

'Well, well, well. I bet you never thought you'd be seeing me again,' he said with a grin.

Gabby was in a state of utter panic.

'Er, listen, I'm really, really sorry about your boat and, er, deceiving you but . . . it was an emergency,' she said, stuttering out the words.

He was a good looking man she thought to herself yet again, as a feeling she'd never felt before stirred deep inside her.

He held out his hand and she, quite naturally, took it. Marshy glanced up from unloading his boat, shook his head and smiled.

They sat on a big flat rock, formerly part of a Druid's altar, as the locals of Connemara liked to call them, or megalithic tomb, to use the official term. They were ancient burial sites dotted all around the west.

'Tell me I didn't see you flying from the sinking boat,' he said to Gabby as she regained her composure.

'You didn't see me flying from a sinking boat,' she said unsmiling staring into his deep brown eyes.

'Carrying a dog?' he added.

Gabby held her hands together on her lap and lowered her head as if to study them.

'Nope, not me,' she whispered softly.

Impressed by her demeanour and seemingly genuine gentleness, he decided not to force the issue.

'Come on, CJ, give us a hand here. There'll be plenty of time for chatting later,' Mo Mo shouted, lifting a case of beer onto her shoulder.

They all lent a hand and quickly the little tractor and trailer were full of supplies. CJ drove, as they all followed along behind toward the house.

Gabby had noticed the animated conversation between mother and daughter, quite aware she was the subject being discussed. As they neared the cottage Mo Mo pulled her aside.

'Gabby, I have some news for you. Your mother is still alive.'

'What? How is that possible? I was holding her in my arms when she was shot. She's dead,' said the girl, tears welling up in her eyes.

'She can't be alive, can she?' she asked, hopefully, gripping Mo Mo's sleeve.

'She's in a protective ward at Galway Regional Hospital. She's going to be okay,' Mo Mo said, grinning.

Gabby threw her arms around the older woman's shoulders, tears flowing down her cheeks.

'I can't believe it, are you really, really honestly sure she's okay?' Gabby asked pulling back, wiping her eyes with the back of her hand and looking deep into Mo Mo's face for any sign of betrayal. There was none. Mo Mo could only nod and smile.

'Yes dear, we're sure,' she said.

Overcome with so much emotion and happiness, Gabby temporarily forgot where she was. She ran down the pathway laughing and screaming with delight, extending her wings and leaping up into the sky. Jack stood barking. Henry and Perdita were silent, not sure what to make of the giant winged creature. Mo Mo, Jane, Crabapple and Marshy were too stunned to utter a single syllable.

She flew spiralling up to around 1,000 feet before turning and dropping like a stone with wings tucked in. Just at the last second, as if to show off, she deployed them once more causing ripples on the calm surface of the bay. She hovered there smiling and laughing ecstatically until she noticed the dumbfounded looks on the four humans, two birds and a dog.

Jones and Marshy were trying hard not to stare at the contours of her lithe body. Although covered in millions of tiny feathers, it still left little for the imagination of the two healthy young men.

'What?' she said folding her arms across her chest, wings beating slow and methodically.

'Never seen a flying girl?' she said showing a slight grin.

'Many times,' said CJ, laughing.

Gabriella floated over the dock and landed beside him, retracting her beautiful plumage once more. She leaned forward and kissed him very gently on the lips. His eyes opened wide in surprise.

'What was that for?' he asked. She turned and took Mo Mo's hand.

'That was for lending me your boat that wasn't actually yours to lend,' she said, tossing her hair as teenagers do.

'Hey wait a minute. I didn't lend it to you, you stole it,' said Jones.

Gabby looked back and said, 'Borrowed it, I borrowed it. Got to go now.'

CJ was speechless as the three women marched up toward the house, Gabby pulling on her jacket as her feathers began to dissipate under her skin.

The boys were still unloading the boat as Mo Mo and Gabriella sat down in her bedroom, Jack curled up at her feet. The roof was closed so they could hear themselves talk.

'So my father raped my mother and her hair turned white. How can that be?' she asked.

'It was basically the trauma of the event. It's a rare occurrence but has been known to happen before in other cases.'

'So, after the assault?'

'As your mother reached full term we started to hear the rumours.'

'The rumours . . . about me?'

'Yes. Your grandfather still knew people he could trust. So he sent them to *The Festival of the Gypsies*, where the incident took place, to find out who was responsible. It was then the stories began to surface about an evil old woman called Scafa, the leader of your father's clan, who had sworn her grandson's death would be avenged,' said Mo Mo.

'But that's not the only reason for this blood feud is it?'

'No, darling, because you were born a girl this Scafa is convinced you will bring destruction to her and curse her family forever.'

'Just because I'm a girl?'

'No, not just that. It's because you're the first born of the seventh son of the seventh son.'

Jane knocked and entered the room.

'Is it okay if I sit in?' she asked.

'Fine with me,' said Gabby. Mo Mo nodded.

'But didn't my grandfather also kill the two men responsible for my . . . er . . . conception?'

'Indeed, Malut your father and Boris his brother.'

Gabby was trying to unravel everything.

'How many people know about me and what I can do?' she asked.

Jane spoke next, 'Well, the three of us and the two boys, the two assassins, one of which I killed, the woman who leads the clan and we think another man equally as dangerous.'

Gabby and Mo Mo's eyes opened wide in disbelief both asking the same question at exactly the same time,

'You killed one of the assassins?'

'Well, someone else had started the job for me,' she said, looking at Gabby.

'Explain please, mother' said Mo Mo.

'Someone had cut her hand cleanly off. I just helped her along.'

The two elder women looked at Gabby.

'Oh her. She and a baldy little French guy had me tied up and drugged in a van. I had to do something,' said Gabby casually.

'So you sliced off her hand?' asked Mo Mo, horrified.

'She stuck a knife in me. What did you expect me to do, laugh?' said Gabby, deciding not to mention the man whose head she'd removed.

'I'm not scared anymore. I've got my own bunch of assassins right here,' said Mo Mo, beginning to laugh.

Pretty soon they were all rolling around on the bed laughing hysterically.

After a few minutes Jane stood.

'I noticed the leading edge of your wings is made of some kind of metal or something. What's that about?' she asked.

Gabby shrugged and looked to Mo Mo for help. Mo Mo thought for a moment before replying.

'I believe the metal could possibly be a titanium and iron mix, from the two types of blood in your system.'

'Huh?' said Gabby

'Please explain,' Jane asked.

Mo Mo stood and walked around the bed, thinking.

'Well, your mother mentioned that your father's clan - the Menjanii I think she said - were, for generations before the criminal enterprises of today, miners in the south western regions of Romania. Titanium mines to be precise.'

'Yes, I heard that, go on,' said Gabby fascinated.

'Well, your family has, for generations, always lived around Connemara.'

'Still not getting it' said Jane.

'I know. The iron rich water around the west of Ireland has somehow mixed with the titanium, inside me. Am I right?' asked Gabby

'Right, forming some type of metal alloy. At least it's an explanation,' added Mo Mo.

'Why wouldn't her whole body have it then?' Jane asked skeptically

'I don't know Mum. I'm not as smart as you,' Mo Mo said coolly, opening the door.

'Hey, you two. Be nice okay?' said Gabby staying in her room as Jane followed her daughter out.

CHAPTER 23

Binky McFarland's plan was that after his trip around the islands of Britain and Ireland, he would write a book on his adventure. He'd retired from journalism the previous year at the young age of fifty. He just didn't like the direction the print media was headed. All sensationalism these days he'd told his wife. She'd said *no job*, no stay and she'd left him for greener pastures in Australia. Their marriage had never been very solid. He'd not missed her much.

He was still walking around in a haze after the encounter with the flying girl. He couldn't get her out of his mind. Although he'd promised her he would never say anything to anybody, the journalist in him was having a tough time dealing with it.

Two days after the collision he decided to go to the police station in Clifden and see if anything unusual was taking place in the area. For all he knew, the police might say:

Ah yeah, sure isn't that Maggie, Paddy's daughter the flyin' lass.

This he seriously doubted. Binky pushed down on the door handle and nothing happened. He looked around to see if there was another entrance to the station.

'Very strange,' he said to himself, remembering this was the west of Ireland where time ran its own course. He tried it again, banging on it the second time. Nothing.

Garda Shanahan knew he had to do something . . . and quick. Although bound and gagged, the policeman had an incredible will to live. Getting weaker and weaker, through pure stubbornness and thoughts of revenge, he'd managed after thirty minutes, to shimmy the chair across the blood-soaked floor to the window. By twisting his neck he could now see outside into the car park. Only his car remained. Sitting up straight once more he knew he had limited options.

Shanahan was blacking out. The severe amount of blood loss was taking his life. He was fighting hard to stay conscious. Then he thought he heard banging on the front door.

It happened again, he wasn't imagining it. He knew he had it in him to make one last effort. He managed to lift himself and the chair several inches off the floor and with super human strength he smashed the back of his head against the glass. Being tempered glass there was hardly a mark.

Binky had decided to come back tomorrow and was walking past the side window of the station when he heard a *thunk* of something hitting the glass. All he saw was the back of somebody's head disappearing from view. He pulled up a cement block that was lying on the ground and peered inside.

Shanahan twisted his now bleeding head around and much to his relief, he saw a pair of glasses looking in at him.

Binky fished out his mobile phone. No coverage. He cursed out loud and then spotted some workmen leaning on shovels across the road.

'Help!' he said waving and running.

'I need your help.'

The three men looked at him like he was mad. One pointed at the Garda station and said smugly,

'You're going the wrong way.' They all laughed.

'You need to help me break in. There's a man in trouble,' Binky said panting, hands on knees.

The three workmen looked at him and then each other.

Another said, 'There'll be three men in trouble if we help you.'

They all laughed together.

Binky searched the ground and the open van with his eyes. Then he saw what he needed. He grabbed the sledgehammer and ran as fast as his stubby legs could carry him. The workmen strode after him shouting and cursing.

To any onlookers it would have seemed comical. Short chubby man slams heavy sledgehammer into garda station window. Short chubby man bounces back off glass, landing on his ass.

Two of the workers pulled Binky to his feet while the other had the foresight to look through the window. He grabbed the hammer and powered it through the glass, shattering it into a thousand pieces.

Another man, smaller and slimmer than the rest, scooted through and he unlocked the door.

Shanahan was in a bad way and so rather than making room in the work truck, the stronger two carried him in a 'fireman's lift' and ran across the street and up the short hill to the hospital.

CHAPTER 24

After twenty four hours in the hospital Garda Mark Shanahan checked out. He wanted to thank his rescuer and so went over to The Station House Hotel to seek him out.

Binky was sitting in the bar having a pint and a sandwich. Upon seeing Shanahan he stood and offered him his arm. The man was still somewhat unsteady on his feet.

'Binky McFarland,' he said, extending his hand.

Mark clasped it and nodded concentrating more on sitting down without falling on the floor. Once settled he grinned and picked up a menu.

'Anything good here?' he asked.

'Everything I've tried over the past few days has been excellent' smiled Binky.

'How are you feeling?'

'Much better thanks to you. May I ask you a question?' said Mark while signalling to the waitress.

'Of course you may.'

'Why did you need to see me?'

'Well, it's all a bit weird actually. I was hoping you could tell me if anything strange has been happening around here recently?'

'Strange? In what way?'

'Odd, unusual, bizarre.'

'Why do you want to know?'

'Em, well, something amazing happened to me the other day and being a retired journalist, let's just say, my interest was piqued.'

'What happened?'

'I can't tell you.'

'I'm sure you can really.'

'No, I really can't.'

Shanahan leaned forward, elbows on the table,

'Did someone threaten you?'

'Oh no, nothing like that. I promised, that's all.'

'I'm a member of An Garda Siochána. I think you can trust me you know.'

Binky wasn't sure what to do next and so he reasoned a compromise would be okay.

'I met an unusual girl carrying a dog. That's all. You won't get any more, so don't even try.'

Shanahan sat back in his chair pondering the possibilities of what could be so weird or strange about meeting a girl and her dog.

'In what way was she unusual?'

'Well, she had incredible almost unnatural eyes,' he said, thinking to himself, *and silvery claws and brilliant white wings and she saved my life* but he didn't say any of that.

Shanahan leaned forward once more deciding to start small with the questions.

'What kind of a dog was it?'

Binky was relieved the policeman hadn't pushed him further on the girl.

'Oh, a bloodhound, I think.'

'Are you sure?' Shanahan asked, his mind already going back to his missing partner, Sheila, and his suspicion that she was one of the killers who visited the vet. The description Jane had given him was almost identical.

'I'm sure. I know my dogs.'

Shanahan's mind was in overdrive. Jasper, Sheila's bloodhound, must be the dog Binky had seen. He'd never seen another in these parts. So what was an *amazing girl with strange eyes* doing with it?

'Where was this girl?'

'No, no, no. I promised her. Besides, you wouldn't believe me anyway.'

'Try me.'

'Obviously something has been happening around here. If you tell me what it is, I might be able to tell you more about the girl, okay?'

Shanahan thought for a moment before replying.

'A week ago there was a fire fight at a campsite used by local travellers. Many were killed but nobody was caught.'

'Any escape?'

'We think a girl was the target and we think she escaped, but nothing is certain at this point.'

'You have a description of the girl?'

'Not really. We think she's about five foot nine with light brown skin, and bright red hair.'

'Not the girl I saw. Mine had long white hair.'

'It might have been a wig you know.'

Binky didn't need to think long about that. The girl had been flying at tremendous speed, no wig, no way.

'No, it was not a wig,' he said as he stood and threw some cash onto the table.

'If I think of anything else I'll call you.'

Shanahan nodded, he didn't have a choice.

CHAPTER 25

Gabby, Mo Mo and Jane were sitting out in the garden talking about future plans. CJ and Marshy had left several hours before, after being warned by the women to be extra careful around strangers and certainly not to talk to anyone about anything they'd seen. Perdita and Henry were nuzzling against Gabby's hair, one on each shoulder. Jack was lying at Gabby's feet twitching and dreaming and letting flow odorous wind. After one particular long and smelly fart, Gabby had had enough. She stood and looked at Mo Mo.

'Must fly, wind is getting up.'

Mo Mo smiled, 'Go ahead, we'll let you know what we discuss.'

Gabby smiled back, faced them both and let her robe drop to the grass. Her hair was already turning white, her eyes changed colour and the tiny feathers were out along with her long talons. Her face seemed to change shape becoming more aerodynamic. She turned away as the huge white wings unfurled themselves from her back and between her shoulder blades beating slowly.

Mo Mo put her hand up to her mouth, tiny tears running down her cheeks. Jane was similarly affected by the transition. Although both had seen her fly, they were overwhelmed to see it all happen so beautifully, right in front of them.

'Oh, don't worry. I'll be able to hear you. When my body changes, so do my senses.'

With that, she lifted off the grass, staying under the canopy, wings beating lazily. Perdita and Henry flew with her alternatively landing on her legs and wings, squawking uncontrollably with excitement. Every time the threesome flew by, Jack would howl like a wolf baying at the moon.

Gabby stopped suddenly, hovering above Mo Mo.

'What about my mother?'

The two older women look at each other conspiratorially.

'We were just saying that we think we should bring Caitlan here to the island. We don't think she'll remain safe in Galway considering all that's going on.'

'What do you think, Gabby?' added Jane.

'I agree. Do you want me to go get her?'

'No. Too dangerous. After all, it is you they want,' said Jane.

'We do need you to do something before we go, if you're up for it, of course,' Mo Mo said.

'Sure, what do you need?'

Jane cleared her throat.

'Only if you think it's safe, we think someone should check out the Frenchman on Morag's Revenge. If what the boys said is true, he is probably marooned there and, therefore, no threat to us, on our upcoming journey to Galway.'

'Just be extremely careful. You don't need to land there. You should be able to see him from a distance, yes?' asked Mo Mo.

'I'll be fine. Should I . . . er . . . incapacitate him if he's there?' she said in all seriousness.

Jane and Mo Mo looked at each other in horror.

'No no, don't . . . er . . . hurt him at all.'

'Oh lord no!' said Jane, glancing toward the girl.

'Oh you little sh . . .' she said laughing, realizing she'd been played.

Gabby was still laughing as she pumped her wings and shot out from under the canopy into the chilly morning mist. It took her only twenty minutes to get to Morag's Revenge, flying high above the cloud cover and then skimming the waves. She flew over the superstructure of a ruined old trawler floundering on the black rocks. Her eyesight and hearing were fully attuned to anything and everything. She saw no sign of the little bald man as Jane had called him, until she glided over the cliff edge and saw him on the rocks below.

She watched him from high above, for several minutes, still uncertain if the nearly imperceptible movements were caused by the tide or him in the throes of death. She hovered closer. He opened one eye, the other was clearly missing.

'*Mon Dieu*, it is you Gabriella,' he croaked, his body smashed and broken.

'It is me. You are dying, Frenchie, so now you can tell me who's after me.'

'You are right. These are bad people, Gabriella, very bad. 'His name is Visnik. He runs a priory in northern Spain above San Sebastian. He wants to capture you for medical experiments. She, on the other hand, is much more dangerous. She just wants you dead. Her name is Scafa and she is your great gra . . . .'

It was all the Frenchman had left. He struggled to say more but couldn't.

Seconds later he was dead.

Gabby pondered what the dead assassin had said for a while before gliding down and picking him up, carrying him up over the cliffs. She set his body down beside a cave and then, after retracting her wings, pulled him inside. She reasoned it was better for him to disappear altogether than be found floating in the sea. Besides, it seemed the right thing to do.

CHAPTER 26

Visnik and Scafa had finished examining the vet's house for any signs of the woman or Visnik's missing assassins. Shanahan had eventually told them what had happened at the vet's home according to the woman herself.

He'd said there had been no sign of the body of the killer, Sheila. However, they must have come here for one reason only: to get treatment for the sliced off hand.

'Who would cut off someone's hand?' Visnik asked himself, as Scafa froze, deep in thought.

There was one clue that revealed itself upon searching the place: a framed photograph of a mother and daughter hugging in a tropical paradise somewhere.

Before Visnik could start the rental car, there was a series of pinging sounds from his phone. He listened twice before turning to Scafa.

'It appears only one of my people, the man, spoke to someone called McBride two days ago, hired him and his boat for a mission to search some islands off the coast. Neither has been seen or heard from since.'

'Was that Morse code?' she asked after listening to the beeps.

'Indeed it was. For security reasons. Not many people use it anymore. Now, we need to make plans.'

The photograph had the name of the photographer in Galway and so Visnik would go to visit him and Scafa would go to the hospital to persuade the survivor of the campsite fiasco to help in locating the girl Gabriella.

Visnik and Scafa parked the stolen car behind the cathedral. As well as his satellite phone using only Morse code, he and Scafa had purchased two 'throw away' mobile phones for local communications. Visnik walked to Shop Street and Scafa toward the hospital, each only ten minutes away.

On Shop Street, Visnik had found Simon Rowley's photo gallery. A tiny bell rang as he entered startling him. Visnik was unused to the niceties of modern life. He was a cold and brutal man.

A shapely young woman sat behind a clean mahogany desk.

'May I help you?' she asked, dropping any thoughts of adding the 'Sir' after one look at his face.

Visnik removed the photo he'd stolen from the vet's home.

'Where was this taken?' he asked brusquely.

Before she could answer, an older gentleman came through the hanging curtain dividing the shop. Simon Rowley was used to dealing with the public, but he sensed this man was not your average client. He took one look at Nicole, his assistant, and could see she was nervous.

'Why don't you go get your lunch, dear, while I take care of Mr . . . ?'

Visnik produced an evil looking curved knife a bit like a miniature Scimitar. He grabbed the girl by the hair while flipping the closed sign over on the door.

'Get into the back room! Now!' he screamed pushing the girl in front of him.

There was a couch and small kitchenette and a door leading to the dark room with a red light above to signify when in use.

'Sit down and shut up!' he shouted, pushing Nicole down and checking the darkroom for anyone else. He ripped the phone line out of the wall and told the girl to bind Simon's hands and feet. Once done he removed two garbage bag plastic ties and did the same to her.

Jane and Mo Mo were driving through the outskirts of Galway, heading for the hospital when Jane said,

'We should call into Simon's.'

Mo Mo glanced at her watch, then looked at her mother.

'We could do it now before seeing Caitlan. Doesn't he usually go off shooting in the afternoons?'

'Usually yes, but then there's nothing usual about Mr. Rowley. .' she said.

'Fine by me, we'll surprise him.'

They found a space in Middle Street, parked the car and walked up Shop Street to the studio. The pedestrian-only road was busy with bustling bodies rushing to lunch in every direction.

A large man in a black robe, with an acne-scarred face, barged right between them, knocking Jane to the ground. Luckily Mo Mo had just grabbed her mother's hand to prevent separation in the crowds and so the damage was more embarrassment than physical.

'Hey you!' yelled Mo Mo after the disappearing figure.

'Bastard!' added her mother.

As they neared the shop Mo Mo spotted the *Closed* sign on the door.

'Looks like we missed him,' she said.

'Rubbish. He forgets to flip it half the time,' said Jane pushing inside the unlocked door.

'Simon! It's your lover! Ha ha!' she said winking at her daughter.

Mo Mo sniffed the air several times before recognizing the smell of fire. She ran through the curtains searching for the source. Opening the dark room door she was shocked to see reels of film ablaze but more surprised to see Rowley and a girl tied hand and foot, mouths taped shut.

'Mum, help me here!'

The two women sliced through the bonds with razor blades they found on the framing desk and pulled them outside coughing and wheezing.

'Call the Fire Brigade!' Simon said as he fought to get his breath while staunching a deep cut on his hand. 'Bastard cut off my finger!'

As Mo Mo comforted the young woman, Simon whispered urgently to Jane,

'He wanted to know where I took the photo of you and Mo Mo. I had to tell him . . . he . . . was going to torture the girl next.'

Jane grabbed her daughter and said,

'You've got to call the radio service and send a message to the island. No codes in case Jones has gone and Gabby's alone.'

'Hang on mum, I'm calling the fire . . .'

Jane snatched the phone, hung up and thrust it back into Mo Mo's hand.

'Call the island! He's after Gabby!'

She turned to the passersby and screamed,

'Would somebody call the fire brigade, please!'

Mo Mo dialled up the Cleggan Marine Service but there was nobody there only an answering machine. She left a message.

'Call me back Paulie, it's Mo Mo Kelly, emergency!'

After a few minutes had passed the police and fire service arrived but before they could tend to Simon's hand Mo Mo had pulled him aside.

'What did the person who did this to you look like?'

'Tall, scarred face wearing a black robe and sandals, had a foreign accent, maybe eastern European somewhere.'

Jane heard the end of the conversation.

'Crap!'

'Mother!'

'Oh stop it. My generation invented the word, crap, crap, crap!'

'What was he saying?' asked Mo Mo as Simon sat in the ambulance.

'From what Gabby told us yesterday, the two assassins who captured her and then visited me, mentioned a name which sounded like Vinnick or a similar sounding name when they had her in the van. They were very scared of him apparently'.

Call the guards! Tell them!' Mo Mo added.

'Oh please! Even if they believed us, what do you think the odds are they'd find him or get to the island on time?'

'True I suppose. Besides, I don't think we need any more people knowing about Gabby's abilities.'

'So, we'll have to find him and stop him ourselves.'

'The hospital! Bet you he's gone to the hospital.'

Jane ran over and kissed Simon on the cheek.

'Look after yourself, Simon, and make yourself scarce for a while, will you?'

He nodded, still a bit dazed as the two women ran back down the street to their car.

CHAPTER 27

University College Hospital, Galway was a huge, sprawling mass of conjoined buildings. Caitlan was housed in a small single bedroom at the end of the jail wing on the top floor. The powers that be had decided it was the best place for her own security. She was, after all, the only survivor of a brutal attack.

Shanahan had contacted his superiors with the whole story as he knew it so far. They had been typically bureaucratic and sceptical but had agreed that there might be a greater threat to Caitlan O'Toole and so had increased the Garda presence at the hospital to two officers.

She'd been moved from intensive care earlier that morning after the bullet had been removed from her chest cavity. She had lost a lot of blood but the prognosis was now good and the burns would heal in time.

Scafa was a patient woman. She sat for two hours in the main waiting room on the top floor just watching the world go by. A couple of people had asked her who she was visiting but after speaking a few guttural sentences in Albanian they quickly moved on.

Scafa spoke six languages well and several more dialects of each. She was a cunning old hag who was a brilliant manipulator of minds. She was dressed in peasant garb: a thick cotton ankle length dress of drab colour and a heavy, black shawl, common throughout Ireland in days gone by.

She always blended in with her surroundings. This was how she'd stayed alive all these years. She was flicking through one of those awful tabloid magazines that seem to spring up out of nowhere in waiting rooms around the world, when suddenly she saw someone she didn't expect. It was the woman from the photo they'd taken from the vet's house. Jane was standing at the nurses' station talking to a police sergeant.

Scafa got up slowly and moved to the lifts, pressing the call button while keeping an eye on the vet. The woman was gesticulating crazily. When the doors closed behind her Scafa texted Visnik. He was already half way to Cleggan in a rental, driving like a man possessed, which she thought he probably was.

Jane ran into Caitlan's room, held her hand briefly and said they had to get back. Caitlan nodded not quite understanding, still in the throes of large doses of pain medication. Jane rushed past the garda and back down the stairs.

Mo Mo was parked in the two minute only parking section, her eyes focused hard on the front doors of the hospital.

'Come on mother! We have to go!' she mumbled to herself as an old woman shuffled out with eyes darting subtly in every direction.

Scafa scanned the doctors' car park for suitable transportation. She spotted a brand new Jaguar V12 E-type, decided she wanted it and took it without difficulty. Scafa had stolen her first car at the ripe old age of ten.

The ancient looking woman got in a brand new purple-coloured Jag, surprising Mo Mo, as she peeled out of the car park with screeching tyres, barely missing several pedestrians.

'Wow! Crazy bitch!' she said, opening her mouth in mock horror.

'Good way to catch flies,' said Jane as she jumped into the passenger seat, buckling up and looking at her daughter expectantly.

'Any messages from Paulie?'

Mo Mo started the car and pulled out into traffic heading for the road to Cleggan.

'No, nothing yet.'

CHAPTER 28

Upon her return to the island Gabby discovered Mo Mo and Jane had left for Galway. She knew this because CJ had bought over a speedboat and changed places with the women. Having him stay with her was only comforting in the sense she was attracted to him. *He could hardly be there to protect me* she thought to herself.

CJ was lying on the couch reading a magazine when Gabriella descended the staircase after a nap and a shower. She was wearing a knee length white cotton dress and drying her hair knowing full well he was watching her.

'What are you reading?' she asked.

He held it up so she could read the title.

'National Geographic? Ah ha, also known as the Irish Playboy.'

'Funny, you're very funny,' he said drolly.

'You know that's where most people in Ireland learned about the human body before the Internet and them smut mags?' she said, lightly touching the kettle making sure it was hot.

'I heard the same stories so you're not as original as you might think,' he said flicking through the pages

'Tea?'

'Please,' he answered.

'Oh but I am original, don't you think?' she said pouring the water into two large mugs.

'I meant mentally not physically.'

'Oh, I think I'm the smartest person around here,' she said with a teasing smirk, handing him the mug. He blew once and took a sip.

'That's doubtful.'

'Oh, you're just threatened by my female superiority.'

'No, that's not it.'

'Then tell me why?'

'Well, most people, with even half a brain, would put a teabag in a cup of tea for starters,' he said grinning, as she took away his mug returning to the kitchen.

'Your amazing mind must have been distracted by something. I wonder what it was?' Jones said with a huge smile on his face.

She glanced back at him in obvious embarrassment.

'You men, honestly, you think you're God's gift to women,' she said handing him back the tea.

'We aren't? I could have sworn my da . . .' she stopped him talking by placing her hand over his mouth.

'Oh please, give it a rest,' she said with a sigh.

'I have an idea. Let me show you all around the island after our tea. It's beautiful out there and I think we could both use some air, okay?'

She knew immediately it was something she would like to do and so nodded her consent.

'Okay.'

They left the house, Gabby carrying a picnic lunch she had hastily thrown together and Jones a blanket. They were both thinking the same thing and asking themselves the same question. *What was going to happen after the food was gone?* Meanwhile the house phone rang and rang with nobody there to answer it.

Kelly's island was all bluffs and cliffs except for the

hidden bay, but inland, outside the canopy, there was still plenty for Gabby to marvel at.

She'd only ever seen rabbits cooking over the spit but now there were hundreds of them running around, diving into their burrows when approached. Gabby was smiling and obviously so enamoured by this that CJ found himself smiling with her.

Wild flowers carpeted much of the island with stunningly beautiful butterflies flitting and landing everywhere.

'What a magical place,' she said to Jones, gently leaning on his arm.

'Tis that alright,' he replied, trying hard to think of just the butterflies.

On they walked, Gabby like a little child seeing everything for the first time. They stopped at a small bog pool. As Jones picked up a stick, Gabby bent down and cupped out some water. After sipping it she said,

'That's almost sweet.'

'Aye, it's the frogeepee that makes it so,' he said, trying hard not to laugh.

'Frogeepee? What's that, some kind of plant?' she asked so innocently he almost nodded.

'No. Frog piss,' he said laughing as she tried to spit out what she'd just drunk.

Then she turned on him, swinging at him with the picnic basket.

'Dick! You could have stopped me!' she said, smiling as she chased after him backtracking through the flowers.

'*Oh, it's so sweet!*' he said, mimicking her and laughing hard.

Whether he tripped on purpose or accidently never came up in later conversation, but he landed hard on the grass a few feet away with her tumbling on top him.

'You know, if I wasn't such a nice person I could kill you,' she said grinning.

'Who told you that?' he asked softly.

'You've seen what I can do. You'd better behave,' said a smiling Gabby, leaning forward over him, her legs astride his thighs.

'No, I meant who told you, you were nice?'

He raised up his legs and tossed her over beside him, quickly holding her arms to her sides. This time she didn't fight him. They looked searchingly into each other's eyes, their mouths getting closer until their lips touched ever so softly. Gabby gently wrapped her hands around his neck pulling him down, their lips locked together in a body-shaking embrace.

After several minutes of nearly removing each other's tonsils, he moved down to her neck, barely tickling the tiny red hairs with his lips. He was slow and patient, knowing full well she was getting more and more excited by his teasing touch.

He eased his left leg over hers until he was half on top of her. This gave him more neck surface to caress with his tongue. He moved his left hand onto her right breast gently at first but then once the nipple became visible through the sheer cotton he moved his fingers with more definition. Gabby arched her back softly, moaning his name as she entered the throes of frenzy.

Between kissing her hard on the lips and gently probing the hollow at the front of her neck with his tongue, while softly massaging the lobe of her left ear with his right hand, she was reaching a point of ecstasy.

Gabby pushed him upright and began to undo the buttons on his shirt, finally losing patience and ripping them off. He unhooked the clasp at the back of her neck and pulled down the top of her dress.

Two minutes later they were both naked and moaning in the heat of passion between two people who so totally transcended the level of just wanting sex. Their lovemaking was fulfilling and complete and so after twenty minutes they both lay back on the grass exhausted, staring up at billowing clouds.

Gabriella propped herself up on one elbow and stared into his brown eyes.

'Not bad . . . for a fisherman,' she said smiling.

'Okay . . . for a traveller,' he said, with a huge grin, moving his right arm under her elegant neck.

She said, 'Could you, being a gentleman and all, go and fetch the blanket you seem to have dropped over there, please?'

He glanced over, shook his head and lay back down pulling her closer.

'Naw, I'm fine. You'll keep me warm enough.'

She snuggled in beside him.

'You're a lazy git you know?'

'Ah sure, I'll bet you weren't thinking that a few minutes ago,' he said.

Gabby blushed slightly and had to agree.

'Well, I suppose you're right.'

It only took a few seconds of deep concentration on her part before a shadow flitted across his face causing him to quickly open his eyes. It was amazing to watch as her six foot long left wing appeared from under her and ever so gently floated down over the two of them, locking them into a cocoon of warmth.

'Wow!' was all he could utter.

CHAPTER 29

Binky McFarland and Garda Mark Shanahan were standing at the end of Cleggan Pier talking to Patsy, a local fisherman about renting a boat, to seek out the mysterious island where a supposedly even more mysterious girl lived: one who could fly. Shanahan hadn't elaborated on all this to his superiors knowing they would lock him up in a rubber room for ever.

The fisherman was haggling over the price of the rental of his trawler when suddenly Shanahan turned white. The tall robed man who, with the old crone, had left him to die, was striding down the pier toward them. He hadn't seen them yet. He was more interested in looking at boats either for rent or for stealing.

'Patsy, can we look inside?' Shanahan said grabbing hold of Binky's jacket and pulling him down the gangplank and onto the trawler.

'Well, I . . . .' said Patsy stroking his chin as the two men disappeared inside.

As he turned he was confronted by a large foul-smelling man in a black cassock.

'I need boat!' said Visnik

'No boats here. Why don't ye just piss off ye filthy

bastard?' said Patsy with a big grin on his face.

Visnik was stunned by the reply not quite able to comprehend what the man had just said to him, but understanding the threat. Patsy stood there smiling up at the scarred contorted face.

'Nobody speaks to me that way! I take your boat, but first I kill you!' spat Visnik.

'No, son. Calm down. There'll be no killing here,' Patsy said focusing on his three sons standing behind the monk, two carrying fish hooks and the other a filleting knife.

Visnik turned and assessed the threat. All he had was his miniature Scimitar knife and his ability to kill in close quarter hand-to-hand combat but this would be too dangerous, even for him. He turned and pointed at the elderly fisherman.

'You be very careful, old man. One day.'

He gathered his robes and strode off back down the pier.

'Lads, go make sure nobody rents anything better than a bathtub with no plug to that creature,' said Patsy as Shanahan and Binky emerged from the boat, his sons striding off after the Monk.

'We'll take it. How much for a couple of days?' asked Binky.

''Tis an urgent matter you say? How urgent?' asked the old man.

'Well, that monk, or whatever he is, is chasing a young girl who's somewhere out on the islands. Thanks to you we may get to her first,' said Mark.

The old fisherman scratched his chin for a few seconds before concluding,

'Sounds important stuff. Just pay for the diesel when you return. Fair enough?'

'You're very kind. Thank you,' stammered Binky, not really sure about this whole adventure.

The garda and the Englishman untied the securing

ropes and powered up the engines, heading out into Cleggan bay.

CHAPTER 30

Scafa was not used to the power of the Jaguar especially on the west Irish roads. As a result she nearly lost control several times. Following the third near death experience she calmed herself and the engine down to a more rational state of movement.

Jane and Mo Mo knew the roads backwards from Galway and, not surprisingly, unknown to both, they were making good progress on the old woman in the Jag. Mo Mo asked her mother if there was anyone else they could trust to call with regards to warning the island of the upcoming maelstrom. Her mother thought hard.

'No, can't think of anyone,' she said just as her phone rang.

Jane spoke for two minutes before hanging up.

'No reply. Paulie's been calling for over an hour now. He's left several messages,' she said wondering where the two had gone and if the monk had found them already.

Mo Mo glanced over at her mother, knowing full well what she was thinking,

'It'll be fine. There's no way anyone has found them or even the island yet. They're probably out exploring.'

'The island? Hardly take this long,' said Jane with a

sigh.

'Not the island necessarily . . .' said Mo Mo, with a grin

Jane looked at her daughter and then promptly did a double take, a bit like Abott and Costello.

'You think?'

'Yeah, I think.'

Losing contact with Visnik had only spurred Scafa on to drive faster. The Connemara roads were unsuitable for a high performance Jaguar, especially one driven by such a maniacal woman. As she approached Recess corner, she screeched to a sudden halt. Fifty yards away were two garda cars, end to end, blocking the road west.

There was a line of traffic at the checkpoint. Jane and Mo Mo looked at each other, expectantly, hoping one would make a decision on what to do next. Jane and her daughter opened the car doors and stood on the edge, enabling them to see down the line to the roadblock.

The Gardaí were making everyone in each car get out and show ID. Scafa was three cars back from it and uncertain as to what she should do.

Mo Mo spotted the Jaguar she'd seen earlier at the hospital. She started running.

'There it is!' she screamed, attracting the attention of one of the cops.

The old woman's hearing was still acute. She glanced in the rearview mirror, spotting some woman running and shouting, gesticulating wildly toward her car. Some of Scafa's enemies had made the mistake of presuming the old woman was slow and out of touch with reality. Much to their detriment. She was far from it. As the garda moved closer, she slammed the Jag into gear while swerving into the oncoming lane. Two cars were heading toward her but quickly pulled over to the side.

Mo Mo leapt back into the car.

'Ma, you might want to get out,' she said excitedly. Jane stared ahead tightening her hands around the seat belt.

'Drive!'

Just as the two oncoming cars nervously made their way back onto the road a second car, Mo Mo's, screeched out in front of them. They quickly pulled back over to the grass verge.

Scafa purposely put the car into a four wheel slide, knocking the approaching garda off his feet and into a hedge. Straightening up, she aimed between the front bumpers of the two stationary police cars. The remaining Gardaí dived away to either side. Scafa sliced her way through rendering both cars inoperable. She sped off through the hills surrounding Lough Inagh.

Just as the policemen were getting to their feet, Mo Mo threaded her way through the carnage, hit the accelerator and ignoring the shouts of the Gardaí, Jane screamed,

'Follow the hag in the Jag!'

The two women laughed nervously.

CHAPTER 31

Visnik had earlier spotted kids down on the beach messing around with a speedboat and skis. Then, he'd decided it would be too risky, what with parents probably close by keeping an eye on their adventurous children, to try to steal the boat. Now was different though. After being removed from the pier, his choices were limited.

Visnik was the personification of evil. He knew he had to draw the teenagers away and keep them distracted enough to enable him to reach the boat, start it, and be heading out to sea before they really knew what was happening.

He easily spotted the children's parent or guardian sitting in her car on the causeway between the sea and the lake. She seemed to be asleep, with an open book on her chest. He snuck into the rear door of the vehicle and before she knew anything he wrapped his right arm around her neck while stifling her screams with his left. She passed out.

The fast yellow speed boat coasted up onto the sand near the end of the beach close to where Visnik sat watching them. As soon as the boat landed the kids jumped out and made their way toward the car.

Visnik slid into the passenger seat and manhandled the woman's body, jamming her right knee against the accelerator and bending her head down under the dashboard. With one quick glance down toward the approaching teens he opened the passenger door and started the engine. He checked once more that the unconscious woman's knee was still firmly in place before ripping the gear into second.

As he slid out of the door, staying low to the ground, the car screeched off down the road a few hundred yards before careering off the roadway and down onto the beach. The children ran shouting behind.

Visnik picked himself up, dusted off his robe and then casually walked down to the speedboat. With little effort he pushed the fibreglass stern back into the water, jumped in and started the motor.

Binky and Shanahan poured over the charts in the wheel house, trying to pinpoint the location of the collision of the hang-glider and girl in order to work out approximately which island she'd been travelling toward. Binky had slowed the trawler considerably, quite sure in the knowledge they were close to where the accident had happened.

Shanahan stood up to stretch his back when he noticed a speedboat coming up on the port side fast. He picked up the binoculars and focused on the driver.

'Crap! Here's trouble. Do you have a gun?' asked Shanahan.

'A gun? No, I don't have a gun, why would you even . . . ?' said Binky following the policeman's gaze. 'Is that who I think . . .?'

'Yes, yes, find a gun. Quick!' Shanahan said, searching the cabinets under the control panel.

Binky calmly dialled a number he'd been given when rescued from the freezing water. It was the number of the Pier Bar where the barman had certainly warmed the cockles of his heart with about eight shots of Irish whiskey.

'Ah Seamus, it's Binky here, would Patsy be about?' he asked. 'Yes, that's the man, thanks.'

Binky held up his hand to Shanahan.

'Patsy, I'm the guy who just borrowed your boat, I was wondering, would there be a gun onboard by any chance?'

'Oh no! I've no intention of shooting anyone. Yes, yes, I'm sure. We seem to have caught a rather large shark and we need to incapacitate it,' Binky said mopping his brow with the back of his hand.

'Indeed? Thank you, Patsy. No, no, all's fine.'

He turned to Shanahan as Visnik came into view.

'Shotgun, under the mattress, in the forward bunkroom.'

Visnik was taking no chances, staying well off the port side, not sure who was aboard the large fishing vessel.

The fifteen year old Whitecrest fishing boat, built in Scotland by a company now defunct, had a couple of unusual features. One was the extremely large 1,000 horsepower twin screw engine and the other was the small, barely discernible, line of portholes just below the deck. There was no actual glass. They were comprised of metal slats. The reasoning behind the latter was ventilation for the powerful diesel.

Shanahan told Binky what he wanted him to do before descending back down below deck. One minute later, with the boat heading for open sea, Binky started to shout and jump up and down on top of the wheel house gesticulating wildly and removing his clothes.

Visnik had always been a curious man. Seeing the little, rotund, bespectacled man acting like a loon more than piqued his interest. He pointed the speedboat toward the trawler while drawing his Glock 9 mil from his robe.

Shanahan slowly slid the old double barrel shotgun between the slats on the forward porthole, levering them apart while watching Visnik circling the trawler, still at great speed. It would be pure luck if he decided to board the port rail, but Shanahan felt he deserved some good fortune after the last few days.

Visnik did indeed slow down on approach to the port side, his eyes burning into Binky while scrutinising his movements. Fifty yards away, forty, thirty . . . Shanahan took aim. Just as he fired the first barrel, the trawler lurched and dropped from the wake Visnik had created by his circling. His shot went wide of the intended target, Visnik's chest, but some pellets did strike his leg.

As soon as Binky heard the shot, he dived below the wheelhouse dragging his shorts and T-shirt behind him.

Shanahan couldn't believe his eyes as Visnik, who had barely flinched when shot, unloaded his clip into the side of the boat, firing like the mad man Shanahan knew him to be.

At twenty yards, Garda Mark Shanahan took aim at the outboard's larger petrol tank that, although hidden, was usually found below the gunwale close to the motor.

Visnik was too busy cursing while trying to reload his weapon to notice the gun projecting from the porthole once more. Shanahan fired his second barrel and his aim was true. The speedboat exploded into a fireball, throwing the mad monk high into the air, robe ablaze.

Binky and Shanahan searched the burning debris still floating on the sea. They found no sign of the monk either dead or alive.

'We'll continue on for an hour or so. It'll be too dark after ten. Okay with you?' asked Shanahan.

'Fine with me. We can always resume our search for the girl at dawn,' Binky replied, scouring the sky with the binoculars.

'Dawn might be too late,' said the policeman bleakly.

CHAPTER 32

Gabby and CJ returned to the house in the early evening, exhausted after the exploration of all things beautiful, as Jones referred to the day's activities. Upon entering, they heard the phone ringing. Gabby ran over and picked it up. She listened more and more intently as the conversation went on, asking questions of the caller with growing consternation. After a few minutes she hung up and turned to Jones.

'Trouble?' he asked

'Oh yeah' she answered.

They were in the middle of a heated argument about leaving the island or staying when the phone rang again. It was Mo Mo. She and Jane had finally convinced the police, after the fire at Rowleys, to be on the lookout for Scafa and the Monk.

'You can't go Gabby. It's too dangerous.'

'If I don't go and try to stop these crazy people, it will be more dangerous for everyone else, don't you think? Besides, I can lead them away from here,' she said.

'You mean, lead them away from me? I'm not a child. I can help.'

Gabby wrapped her arms around his neck, holding him

tight.

'Okay, we'll stay here together. Maybe they won't find us,' she said kissing him softly on the lips.

Gabby and Jones were sitting in front of the blazing fire, holding hands and talking in whispers like young lovers do.

'Can you cook?' Gabby asked standing and stretching.

'What would you like?' was his reply.

'Surprise me,' she said coyly.

'Sure didn't I do that already?'

She slapped his arm playfully.

'Bold thing! I'm going to take a quick shower,' she said as he began to follow, grasping at her arms.

'Can I help?' he asked mischievously.'

'You can help by cooking me some food. Back in a minute,' she said, grinning, as she ran up the stairs.

Once in her bedroom she felt even worse than she had when contemplating her escape. She knew he'd never let her go, willingly. She could overpower him, of course, but she knew she'd never do that.

She climbed out onto the roof deck removing her clothes as she went. The two white cockatoos, Henry and Perdita, flew down from the canopy screeching noisily. Gabby closed the glass roof for fear CJ might hear the ruckus.

Concentrating for seconds only, all four sets of talons appeared in unison with her incredible, now close to seven foot, wings. She moved them gracefully up and down still marvelling at their strength and beauty. With the two birds at her side, a threesome in white shot out from under the canopy soaring up into the darkening skies.

The two cockatoos, Henry and Perdita, had been unable to keep up with Gabby's hectic pace and had turned back to the island. Gabby herself was hovering roughly half a mile away and five thousand feet above the sea when her acute hearing picked up sounds of an engine and men's voices. She could see the boat moving toward Kelly's island at a fair speed. She watched it for a few minutes as it began to slow and the voices became more heated.

'We've got to find her! Think man!' said Shanahan, impatiently.

'I'm thinking, I'm thinking. I'm sure it was here, somewhere around here. It's not easy, she was a powerful presence, both beautiful and very distracting,' was all Binky could say.

'Beautiful and distracting. That really doesn't help much.'

'I know, I know,' Binky said, thoughtfully.

'She'll be dead beautiful if we don't find her soon.'

'Yes, yes, yes, this I understand.'

Gabby remembered the rotund little man with the glasses and funny accent.

'We're going to have to turn back, you know,' said Shanahan.

Binky wasn't listening. He was watching the skies trying to distinguish if the approaching dot of white was something he'd seen before.

'Huh?'

Shanahan turned and followed Binky's line of sight.

'I said . . . .' was all he could utter.

Gabby hovered thirty feet above the two men, gently beating her wings in a reverse motion to keep a safe distance from the still moving boat.

'You lied,' she said ,matter-of-factly, with no anger but a tiny inflection of disappointment in her voice.

Binky looked terribly heartbroken by those two little words.

'I know. I'm truly sorry. But I have good reason. You're in danger,' he said as Shanahan moved forward to get a better look at this apparition.

'He's right, bad people are after you.'

'And you are?' asked Gabby

'He's with me. He's a policeman. We're here to help,' Binky stammered.

Gabriella moved up and down, back and forth effortlessly, finally coming to rest on the forward gunwale. Her long feet talons digging slightly into the soft wood, her wings continued to beat slowly keeping her upright and focused on the two men.

'People have been after me all my life. You're not telling me anything new here,' she said evenly.

Binky and Shanahan were ten feet away, neither quite able to believe they were actually talking to a flying girl. Her long white hair was blowing out behind her, her green translucent pupils tinged with red, her body covered in millions of tiny white feathers and the edge of her wings reflected the distant full moon's shining light.

Shanahan was the first to speak.

'We know all about you, we came to help. The people seeking you out are pure evil. I know from first-hand experience. Please, let us help.'

Gabby searched their faces, their demeanours, for any sign of danger. She found none.

Before she had lifted off from the roof of Mo Mo's house she had slipped a T-shirt and pair of shorts into the pouches under each of her wings, just in case.

She nodded and asked,

'Please face the other way.'

They did and her talons disappeared as she jumped onto the deck. Her giant wings folded in half and retracted into her back, her hair turned red once more as she slipped on her clothes. She changed back because the energy and strength she needed to fly could be quite overwhelming on her young body.

'Okay, you can turn around now.'

The two grown men could not fathom the transition that had just taken place. She was only a girl, an attractive one at that with amazing powers, but really, only a girl.

CHAPTER 33

Scafa knew she was being followed and she was pretty sure it wasn't the Gardaí who were doing the following. She slowed the Jag and made out an older woman than the driver talking on her mobile phone. Scafa loved modern communications for her various criminal endeavours but hated them in situations like this one.

Anyone could be a cop nowadays. Scafa slowed down even more while she fastened the bracelet tighter to her left wrist. She knew she had full capacity of darts. There was a long straight bit of road ahead so Scafa floored the V-8 engine once more.

'No reception. Bloody mountains!' Jane said, throwing the phone into the back seat.

'Mother, calm down! Besides you love the mountains.'

'Not today,' she said pouting.

They both watched in awe as the Jaguar disappeared around the corner at the end of the straight road.

'Bloody hell! What do we do now?' said Jane.

'Mother, such language!'

'Oh, stop it. Where do you think you learnt it all from?' she said smiling at her daughter.

'We have to follow, no?'

'God, I don't like this. Do you have a gun?'

Mo Mo glanced at her passenger in frustration.

'A gun? Mother, why would I have a gun?'

'In case you ended up chasing some Romany nut cracker. Protection. Didn't I always mention protection?'

'Sexually, maybe, definitely never with regard to my physical safety,' Mo Mo retorted.

'Huh, I thought I did. Sorry about that.'

'What are we going to do?'

'Let's follow her, but be cautious,' Jane said touching her daughter's arm in encouragement.

Scafa pulled over as soon as she rounded the corner, pulling the bonnet release as she exited the car. Listening intently she then unscrewed the radiator cap using her shawl to prevent serious burns to her hand. A fountain of steam and boiling water poured out all over the engine. She slammed the hood down, got back into the car and searched the far side of the road for a suitable spot.

Fifty yards away she drove into the solitary tree, just off the road, head on. She hit at about forty miles an hour, making the desired dent in the front of the Jaguar. That, with the steam still pouring out, made a minor bump look much more serious. Checking her mirrors and opening the electric window on the off side she then struck her head a couple of times on the steering wheel, drawing a little blood. As the women turned the corner, Scafa slumped forward.

Mo Mo skidded to a stop as soon as they rounded the bend.

'Damn!'

'Bollocks!'

'Mother!'

They both stared, wide-eyed, at the crashed Jaguar.

'Any suggestions?' asked Mo Mo of her mother.

'We need a weapon of some kind. What's in the boot?'

'Oh, let me think, we could bop her on the head with the spare tyre, presuming, of course, she'd stay still and presuming this isn't some kind of trap.'

'You're quite the cynic, you know,' said Jane

'Me?'

They both stayed in the car unsure what the situation was in the Jaguar.

'She's not moving,' said Mo Mo.

'Maybe she's dead.'

'We should be so lucky.'

'Drive a bit closer and let's see what's going on.'

Mo Mo scrutinized her mother's face and then slowly pressed the accelerator causing the car to roll forward.

'Release the hood catch,' said Jane.

'You mean the bonnet?'

'Hood, bonnet whatever! The bit at the front that covers the engine.'

'Why?'

'If she starts shooting, it might protect us from being shot,' Jane replied.

So Mo Mo pulled the catch and the old Volvo bonnet sprung open, blocking most of the view but offering some protection to the women. She pointed the car at the Jaguar and crept forward.

'Good idea, unless she has metal piercing rounds of course.'

'Well there is that . . .'

Before she could finish speaking, a tiny metal dart pierced the bonnet of the car and imbedded itself in the thick Plexiglass of the windscreen. Jane and Mo Mo stared at it in disbelief.

'Okay, that's it, we're out of here,' Mo Mo said, ripping the old car into reverse but not before several more darts pierced the engine block causing it to stall out.

Jane caught a wry smile on the old woman's face as she backed out from the tree, waved her shiny arm bracelet and then continued on down the road, leaving them stuck out in the middle of the Inagh Valley, with no traffic and no phone reception.

CHAPTER 34

CJ was dozing on the couch when suddenly the door to the cottage flew open. He leapt toward the fire reaching for the poker,

'It's okay, it's me.' Gabby said with a guilty smile.

He looked at her and then the stairs doing a double take. Before he could say anything two strangers followed Gabby in.

'Shower huh?'

'Crabapple Jones, this is Garda Shanahan and this is Binky, an old acquaintance from days long past.'

'Crabapple? Great first name,' Binky said, trying to lighten the mood.

CJ looked at the two men but made no effort to acknowledge them. He was angry.

'So where did you meet these two? In the shower?'

'Oh stop it and grow up! I had to go and look around. Our lives are in serious danger. Don't you get that?' she said moving to hold his hand.

He started to move away but then realized he was acting like a child. He put his arm around her shoulder and reached forward to shake the two men's hands.

'Good to meet you.'

They all sat down.

'So what's happening?' he asked, concern in his voice.

Shanahan told them the full story, as he knew it, including what they knew about Scafa and Visnik. Gabby filled in the blanks all the way back to the two assassins, one of whom was Sheila, his ex -garda partner.

'That confirms my suspicions,' Shanahan said, putting his hand to his forehead. Just as he was trying to compute all this, the old bloodhound came bounding forward, barking and nuzzling his hand.

'Jasper! You stinky old fella, how are you?' he said bending down only to be bowled over by an odorous whiff.

'Phew eee! Still the same old dog!' he said, laughing.

'Well, not quite. His name is Jack now,' added Gabby, looking fondly at her friend.

'Much better. Jasper always sounded like a butler or something to me.'

'Or a ghost,' chimed in Binky proudly.

Gabby, Shanahan and Jones all looked at each other and mutually decided not to tell him he was probably thinking of Casper.

The four of them sat down to discuss the situation after Shanahan had received an update from the Cleggan Marine Service in connection to the roadblock on the Clifden road.

'It seems our main quarry has evaded the Gardaí, your host and her mother.'

He went on to tell what he had just found out.

'Nobody was hurt?' asked Gabby concerned. 'Just Jane's 1996 Volvo stationwagon.'

'This is neither working nor safe. We have to get to the mainland for many reasons. Firstly, to be able to communicate and, secondly, to make sure no one is heading this way to destroy us all,' said Shanahan.

'I thought you killed the monk. You said you did,' said

CJ.

'We think we did, but we didn't stop to look for his body,' Binky said, impatiently.

'So he could be coming here, or here already, or outside the door listening,' Jones said angrily.

'Stop it all of you. You're like kids. We need to work this out,' Gabby said, calmly.

Everyone was on edge.

Binky, who was sitting beside Gabby, turned and laid his hand on hers but before he could say anything they all noticed her tense up, her eyes flash from red quickly back to green. Binky removed his hand.

'Sorry . . . er . . . I was just going to suggest that some of us men could head back in the boat and you, dear girl, could do your thing from high above. You know? Scan the water and stuff.'

Jones and Shanahan looked at Gabby for any sign of disagreement, but there was none. She placed her hand on his and then stood.

'I think that's a great idea Binky,' she said smiling. 'I have something to take care of first, be back soon.'

'Be back soon? What does that mean exactly?' asked CJ.

Gabby walked over and wrapped her arms around his waist and gave him a long lingering kiss.

'Means I have something to do first. Won't be long,' she said as she skipped out of the door.

CHAPTER 35

Scafa pulled her Jaguar off the road and down an overgrown farm track beside the Clifden to Westport road. She knew it was only a matter of time before the roadblocks were re-established around Cleggan and so she flagged down a motorist, incapacitated her and stole her car. She actually laughed out loud thinking she must be going soft, leaving the two women in the Volvo alive and also the one whose car she was now driving back to Galway, away from the roadblocks.

Forty minutes later she stopped at the side of the road and picked up her satellite phone.

'University College Hospital Galway, can I help you?' said a cheerful voice.

'Yes, how are ya?' Scafa said, mimicking the Irish accent, 'This is Mary from the Galway Animal Rescue. Could I speak with Caitlan O'Toole? She's a patient there.'

There was a slight pause on the line. 'I'm sorry, I have no information regarding that person. Who is this again please?'

'It's Mary, from Animal Rescue. I was told you had a woman there and when her cat was better we were to notify her. Are ya with me?' Scafa said, impatiently.

After the mess at the campsite a report had been issued by the incompetents she'd sent there. Among the items she had gleaned was of a cat leaving the primary caravan with its tail on fire. She knew nothing of the cat's whereabouts now but had always kept that snippet of information in the back of her mind.

'Hold the line please.'

There was a pause for several minutes before the voice came back on.

'I'm sorry, Mary, Miss O'Toole has been transferred.'

The line went dead.

Scafa, always the persistent one, called the hospital back a minute later.

'University College Hospital, can I help you?' came a different voice.

'Caitlan O'Toole, please. It's her Aunt Sarah calling from Boston.'

'Hold the line please,' was the reply.

Minutes later the voice returned.

'I'm sorry, but your niece is no longer here. She's being transferred to The Dublin Burn Centre.'

'Thank you, I'll call her there,' said Scafa, politely.

'Oh, you'll not get her yet. They only left half an hour ago.'

'Thanks again,' she said gunning the engine of the stolen car, heading toward Dublin on the M6.

She was sure she had plenty of time to catch up and allowed herself a small smile in anticipation of having the bitch that caused her grandson's death finally in her hands.

CHAPTER 36

Visnik wasn't dead. He was extremely annoyed. He'd managed to swim to a small spit of rock half a mile from the explosion. It had been one of the most painful things he'd ever had to endure and he was well used to pain. Once up on the rock he'd examined his shoulder. It was seriously dislocated, he was sure Most of his arms and legs were burned. That and the shoulder and the salt water had made him very angry.

He found a suitable fissure in the rockface, inserted his forearm and turned toward the far off islands, bracing himself for the inevitable. The agony he felt was so intense he knew there was only one solution to his two problems. To remain unseen from the girl and numb his shoulder, he jumped into the churning sea once more.

Visnik held his breath for over a minute, clinging onto an underwater ledge to stop from being dashed against the rocks by the breaking waves. He surfaced cautiously. Slowly breathing through his nose, he remained mostly submerged for several minutes before climbing back onto the rock.

He moved his tender shoulder back and forth while gently massaging it. It seemed back in place. Squatting on his haunches he peered off into the distance. Seeing no sign of the girl, he decided to take his chances. He jumped back into the sea and headed to Kelly's Island, knowing it was his only option.

As Shanahan and CJ neared the mainland, Visnik drifted towards the island. He was in a wretched condition. Finally, with the help of a large breaker, he managed to get thrown onto the rocks at the northern end and passed out.

Gabby had been totally preoccupied by so many things recently that she'd only just realized that there was something important she really had to do. So when she took off from Kelly's Island, she hadn't been paying much attention to security issues or honing her acute hearing or long-distance eyesight. It was clear dawn, the sky was brightening quickly and so she climbed higher, belatedly thinking more of her safety and protecting the others.

Gabby was fifteen miles from the island when she found two of the three things she was seeking. The first was a small flock of fulmars flying unhurried two thousand feet above the sea, into which she blended by staying high enough not to spook them. The second was the old oak, the grandmother of trees, still standing proud and tall, near where her life had changed forever.

She continued north at a slow pace She didn't want to be spotted by some avid shooters who might mistake her for a wild goose, a big wild goose, but in the hazy dawn light she felt she couldn't be too careful.

As she neared the site of the conflagration of death which she had so narrowly escaped, the large birds finally scattered in various directions after becoming wary of her presence. She was now quite visible to anyone watching and so she tucked her wings to her side and fell like a rock into the ocean below. She had chosen the hidden bay she knew from when they had camped down the road and skinny dipped in the secluded cove. Retracting her wings and talons just before entry made swimming much easier. As soon as she reached the small beach she dressed herself and moved to the sand dune which she and Sophie, her beloved cat, had been playing on only recently.

Tears started to run down her face. The guilt she now felt was quite overwhelming.

'I'm sorry Sophie, so, so sorry,' she whispered out loud.

She crept forward. Seeing the old campsite in daylight brought home the ferocity of the attack. There was yellow police Do Not Cross tape blowing all around the site. She couldn't really believe there was much investigation still in progress. Her family were travellers after all. 'The plague on humankind' was the way a now retired politician had once put it. She couldn't remember his name and didn't care.

'Sophie! Sophie! Come here girl!' she shouted, her voice breaking with emotional turmoil.

She walked around and around the site, down to the water's edge and back up again calling for her beloved pet. She heard nothing and so decided to change giving herself a greater advantage in hearing and eyesight.

As she concentrated hard, her tiny feathers came through her skin and she slipped off her clothes. Her wings emerged, her talons grew and she became fully aware of all her senses. She ran slowly, beating her wings gently so as not to fly too high off the ground, making herself as unnoticeable as possible. She circled wider and wider out from the destruction calling her name continually.

'Sophie, Sophie, where are you?'

There was nothing for half an hour, until she picked up a sound and honed in on it. It sounded like an animal in pain at the base of the cliffs. With wings now beating hard and fast she reached the sound in seconds.

Twenty feet away and above she spotted her bruised, half-burned and battered cat hanging onto the rockface, two wild dogs snapping and snarling at her little legs.

'Sophie!' she screamed causing all three animals to

briefly turn.

Sophie's eyes widened as she saw something she'd never imagined. It was her chance of escape. Gabby took a second to realize she had probably scared her cat even more than the crazed-looking dogs.

Sophie turned and leapt out over the briefly distracted animals and away down the pathway, followed seconds later by the frothing snarling pit bulls.

Gabriella swooped down, grabbing the two unaware dogs by the scruffs of their necks and without ceremony, but much howling, threw them into the sea below.

Sophie was terrified and was running as fast as her little legs could carry her when all of a sudden she noticed they weren't carrying her anymore. Gabby knew she would try and run again and so held her tight until they found a spit of land with only one escape route. Gabby gently dropped the cat at the far end and flew on ten more feet before pulling back and folding her formidable wings into her back. She slipped on her shorts and T-shirt once more, turning to face her best friend.

'Sophie, Sophie, it's me. Come here, little one. It's okay,' she whispered softly, lying down on her side and scratching the ground in front of her.

Sophie moved quickly around the edge of the small plateau, glancing down while always keeping an eye on the girl before her. She was terrified. The past week had exhausted her weakened body. She had barely eaten and was on constant alert. But there was something familiar about this human. The way she talked and called her name.

After a twenty minute stand-off, Gabby ripped off a piece of her T-shirt, rubbed it in her hands and tossed it toward Sophie. Gabby scooted backwards until they were both equidistant from the cloth.

It took a further half an hour of cautious courage before Sophie finally approached the cloth, still hissing and spitting. She sniffed the piece of T-shirt keeping her eyes firmly focused on Gabby. After several deep inhalations she rolled over on the cloth purring and rubbing her head on it.

Gabby moved forward slowly, crawling along in the dirt, stretching out her hand saying,

'Sophie it's me. It's okay,'

Finally, after what seemed like hours to Gabby, Sophie allowed her back to be stroked, purring like an electric lawn mower as she batted her head against her owner's face and chin.

'Finally!' Gabby said, picking her up. After a couple of minutes she said,

'Now Sophie, this bit might freak you out, but don't worry.'

She left on her T-shirt, reasoning it was already ripped. Her shorts also, knowing she had plenty more on the island and not wanting to risk losing her cat again. With Sophie in a firm two -handed grip, she ran toward the edge of the little plateau, leapt off into thin air while deploying her wings.

She thought she'd soar forward and up but much to her consternation she started getting blown backwards, the westerly winds having strengthened considerably over the past hour. No matter how hard she tried Gabby realized she needed her arms in their wing pouches for strength to get back to her friends.

She landed back on the ground and lifted Sophie up to her face.

'Now, little one, change of plans, okay?'

Sophie's big eyes opened wide and then she batted Gabby's chin once more, seemingly enjoying this whole new game.

Gabby lifted the cat up onto her shoulder where she securely dug her claws into the tiny thick white feathers, her little head nuzzled amongst the long wavy strands of, now white, hair.

Gabby ran once more to the edge, her wings already

wide, her hands inside the pouches. She turned and said,

'Okay Soph, you ready for an adventure?'

There was a faint 'meeow,' blown away in the wind.

With double the strength in her wings and a lot more concentration, she soared upwards with ease. She turned once more to see her passenger wide-eyed, her long white fur nearly being blown off her body. She seemed to be having the time of her life. Gabby laughed as she envisioned landing with a totally bald cat, bits of fur stretched out over the Atlantic.

Once below the cotton wool clouds and with the winds calm, Gabby felt Sophie's little claws relax a bit. So, as she glided onwards she began a slow backward roll allowing her cat to move up onto her chest, while she actually flew upside down. They were head to head Gabby thought, but she couldn't see Sophie's face because the wind was now blowing the fur forward. *She is so cute*, thought Gabby. She removed one hand from under the wing and pushed back the unruly hair.

'You want to do a barrel roll?'

A head butt and a 'meeow' was the response. She seemed completely unperturbed by the fact she was four thousand feet in the air hanging onto a giant bird flying upside down. The difference being, this bird she remembered.

Gabby held onto Sophie with one hand and did the barrel roll. In fact, she did several so that when she straightened up she was quite disorientated. As she righted herself she heard a loud buzzing sound. At the same time she spotted the boat below. She immediately searched the skies and was relieved to see a helicopter heading northwards, away from them.

By the time her eyes had focused once more on the boat, she could see that only two men were on it, instead of three. Suddenly, she realized that she no longer felt Sophie's claws in her back.

'Holy crap!' she exclaimed, spotting her bundle of fluff

dropping toward the ocean at tremendous speed.

Gabby pulled in her wings and dropped downwards, in a state of panic. She knew it was going to be close and so she decided to try kicking her legs to speed up her descent.

It worked and twenty feet above the sea she released her right wing first and scooped Sophie up, pulling her to her chest once more.

'Are you okay?' she said, as she straightened out heading to the boat.

'Meeow meow,' was the reply from Sophie gazing forlornly at the sky above.

'I do believe you want to do that again,' said Gabby clutching her cat before replacing her on her shoulder, feeling the little claws attach to her feathers once more.

Shanahan and CJ were not surprised to see Gabriella land on the deck.

'Where's Binky?' she asked folding her wings down behind her, but not away.

'He decided to stay on the island, said someone should keep an eye on . . . what happened to your shoulder?' asked Shanahan.

'My God, what did you do?' CJ asked, a worried look on his face.

Gabby turned her head slightly and laughed and laughed. The little bump had blended in so well with her feathers and with the wind blowing from behind, no face was visible. She lifted Sophie off her back and presented her to the lads.

'This is Sophie, my cat. I've been so busy recently I just didn't get a chance, so this morning I went and found her,' she said giggling.

'Oh, you're crazy. Yes ma'am, totally bonkers you are,' CJ said, shaking his head in disbelief while walking back to the wheelhouse.

If Gabby was hurt or shocked she didn't show it, thought Shanahan. *This girl is so strong and independent he couldn't imagine anything anyone said could offend her, especially a youngster from the bog end of Connemara.*

'See anyone?' Shanahan asked, concern in his voice.

'Nobody. I'm going to drop off Sophie and then I'll be back. We'll find these people,' she said, turned, opened her wings and off she flew.

CJ watched her go with both worry and longing in his eyes.

Binky was snoring so loudly on the couch when she walked in, that even Henry and Perdita, with their constant cackling and screeching, couldn't wake him. Sophie was mesmerised by the cockatoos but knew in her heart they would never be for her dinner.

Gabby sat on the edge of the couch and gently touched his arm.

'Binky, wake up.'

She noticed a piece of paper in his hand and as she tried to pry it free, he stirred.

'Gabby, you're okay?' he said standing and dusting himself off while still half asleep, taking in the screaming birds and a docile cat. He suddenly remembered he had a note for her and so thrust it into her hand.

'A message from Mo Mo. *Emergency*, the guy said on the radio.'

Gabby read it quickly.

'Binky, stay here please and look after Sophie, my cat, and the others. I've got to go.'

Before he could reply she ran into her bedroom, grabbed some fresh clothes and launched herself off the roof and out through the canopy.

CHAPTER 37

Mo Mo and Jane had got a lift to Leenane, a quaint village at the end of the massive natural fiord known as Killary Harbour. They entered the garda station and went to the front desk.

'May I be of assistance ladies?' asked the lecherous old sergeant with a wink and a nod.

Mo Mo looked at Jane and Jane looked at Mo Mo before rolling her eyes and gesticulating to her daughter to go ahead. Mo Mo leaned forward on the counter, towering over the little man.

'We need to talk to someone maybe a little above your pay grade.'

The intensity in her eyes left little doubt that this woman was not to be messed with.

'Yes Ma'am. Please take a seat,' he said, reaching for the phone.

Ten minutes later a huge ruddy faced man came out and ushered them into a back office. He shook hands with them both and sat down.

'Jack Pollack' he said, pulling out a pen.

'Like the fish?' queried Jane.

'Like the artist?' asked Mo Mo.

He sized them both up, wondering if these two were serious or not.

'Same words, different species altogether,' he said seriously. 'Can I help with something?'

'Yes, sorry, er . . . it's about the roadblock earlier, the woman in the Jag,' said Mo Mo

'Yes?' he said, without expression.

'Well, we followed her and, er , she shot our car.'

Pollack got up, said

'Stay here,' and left the room.

'Now you've done it.' Said Mo Mo.

'Me?'

'Like the fish?'

'Well . . . '

Twenty minutes later the door opened and Pollack entered with two other men. After introductions were made to the two elite 'Special Branch' policemen, they all sat down.

The women related their adventures since the hospital but were shocked to learn of Caitlan's transfer to Dublin.

'Is this normal protocol or did someone special initiate the transfer?' asked Mo Mo somewhat testily.

The men were not used to being talked to like this but reasoned that these two unarmed women had chased down an international criminal mastermind. One of the men called the hospital. There were a lot of one-sided questions and answers before he hung up looking puzzled.

'It's standard procedure. When the patient is strong enough to travel, they move them to a more specialised clinic or hospital,' one of the policemen said.

Mo Mo stared at him unflinchingly.

'So, I presume she has a police escort, being the only survivor?'

They'd decided the fewer people who knew about Gabby, the better. Jane and the other two men looked at the garda who had spoken.

'Er no. We saw no further threat.'

'Idiots!' Jane said, seething.

'Have you ever heard of Caitlan O'Toole's Aunt Sarah?' inquired the other policeman

'Aunt Sarah? No. Why?'

'Well, it seems said person called a couple of hours or so ago asking to speak to Miss O'Toole,' he stated, obviously uncomfortable with the direction the conversation was headed.

'And she said she was Aunt Sarah?' said Mo Mo, exasperated.

'From Boston,' was all the man could say.

'So, let me sum this up. You released a woman, who was shot on a night of carnage during which all of her family died, from the secure wing of the hospital. Then one of the nurses, from said secure wing, told a stranger, from Boston no less, that the patient was on her way to Dublin with no security! Did I get all that right?' Mo Mo said with so much anger and sarcasm she screamed out the last question.

Jane handed her a tissue while patting her back.

'Okay sweetie, deep breaths, we don't want you to have a heart attack.' 'God forbid! Wouldn't know where I might end up.'

The garda who had left the room before the outburst now returned. The three voices became raised before the second special branch officer stood and said,

'Er, we seem to have lost touch with the ambulance carrying your . . . .'

'What . . . ?' Jane said

Mo Mo motioned to the garda for his mobile phone, asked a series of questions, then walked outside dialled and waited,

'Paulie? Yes yes. Please relay this message to the island :

Gabby, your mother is missing in ambulance on way to Dublin. Think they might have her. Ambulance colour green and white, number on roof 372. Be safe, darling. Mo Mo.

You got that Paulie? Good. Thanks.'

Mo Mo and Jane finally relented in their pursuit of Scafa and allowed themselves to return to Cleggan where they were reunited with Shanahan and Jones. They relayed the news from the Special Branch that they would contact the ambulance driver and also send armed patrol cars to intercept it.

'She'll be fine,' Mo Mo said, with little conviction.

Jones was worried sick. There was no news of Gabby. He decided there was little to do, so offered to escort the women back home to the island knowing Gabby would eventually return there, if she was able.

CHAPTER 38

John Miller had been driving emergency vehicles for thirty years. Today was an easy run to Dublin in the old reliable Mercedes ambulance circa 1966. The old girl ran like a charm. The only disadvantage was the radio had never been fixed, but he didn't mind. He enjoyed the peaceful runs to the capital city of Dublin.

There was little traffic on the road which Scafa thought was a plus for her upcoming actions.

'Wouldn't want to hurt too many people,' she said out loud laughing.

Through her cunning and charm she'd discovered the transport vehicle was an old Mercedes, painted green and white.

Ten minutes later she spotted it in the slow lane doing approximately 70 kph. She opened her handbag and brought out a steel container while decreasing her speed. Patience was a virtue she rarely had but right now she chose to exercise it, scanning the rearview mirror until the road behind her was empty.

She opened the box, removing hundreds of tiny spiky ball bearings about the size of a marble. The spikes stopped them rolling too far. They had been made by the same man in Marseilles who'd made her bracelet . He called them 'Bon Bombs'. She started throwing them out of the window. They only detonated when hit with a downward force. Bouncing them off the roadway caused no such worries for Scafa. Any car that ran over them would be instantly incapacitated.

Miller hadn't a care in the world as he listened to Procol Harum on his headset. No traffic, a patient out to the world and the promise of a night in the city, away from the wife. What more could a man ask for?

He was stirred from his musings by a black sedan speeding by, nearly knocking him off the road, just by the turbulence it created.

Jaysus, she must be going 200 kph at least. 'Crazy bitch!' he shouted as she disappeared from sight around a bend.

Scafa checked her seat belt was secure and wrapping the thick old woollen shawl around her head she decelerated slightly before crashing into the central reservation. The car rolled over several times before coming to a stop in the middle of the road, upright, on now shredded tyres. She loosened the straps and unwrapped the shawl before laying her head on the steering wheel.

John Miller came around the bend and stopped fifty feet away. He quickly got out of the ambulance and while rushing forward tried to dial the emergency services. He never did get through. As he fell to the ground he looked back and wondered where all the cars were. That was all he ever wondered.

Scafa covered her bracelet with her sleeve and went over to the dying man. She stared down at him, marvelling at the quickness of the poison. She then took his hands and pulled him alongside her ruined car, reasoning the police might waste valuable time working out the scenario of the accident.

She drove the ambulance off the motorway at the next exit. It mattered little to her where she was. All that mattered was where she was going. Her plan was to drive to Cork, 150 miles south of Dublin, steal a small utility van somewhere along the way and take the next available ferry to northern France. There, she knew, she'd be safe with members of her clan.

First, before any of that, she had to find somewhere deserted so she could make sure her cargo wasn't going anywhere. She pulled off the side road after the town of Shannonbridge and up into a forest of firs. Walking to the rear, she was amazed to see the doors had been padlocked.

'Security' she mumbled out loud 'Ha! I show you security,' she said cackling. She pulled up her sleeve and shot several tungsten darts into the keyhole of the lock. Removing it, she opened the doors.

There were two gurneys in the back. One had every conceivable machine hissing and buzzing and beeping hooked up to it. The other had nothing except a coat and a bag containing some clothes.

Scafa stepped forward and leaning forward was about to remove the oxygen mask to make sure she had the right ambulance when it suddenly it hit her. All she could see were long wavy tresses of red hair.

'It cannot be,' she said out loud, 'Caitlan O'Toole has had white hair since the day of the incident at the festival of gypsies sixteen years ago.'

'Oh, it be! You're not such a *great* grandmother after all.'

Before she could raise her braceleted arm, two hands with talons flashing grabbed her by the throat slamming her against the opposite side of the van. Scafa slid to the floor, staring around the ambulance knowing now the prophecies of death and destruction were true. The creature standing over her was not something she had envisioned even in her wildest imagination.

As she pondered this, Gabby stood back, hair now white, wings unfurled her face jutting forward with blazing eyes.

'Wondering how I got in, aren't you?' she said, moving the leading tip of her right wing and slicing a gash in the side of the van. 'Wonder no more.'

She grabbed the old Romany with one hand and without ceremony flung her out of the open door, sending her crashing into a stone wall some twenty feet away, her body sagging to the ground.

Gabby concentrated hard and returned to her normal self kneeling on the ground while reaching under the gurney. She pulled a conscious Caitlan gently out before lifting her back onto the bed.

'Oh, Mama, are you okay?' she asked.

'Gabriella ,my darling girl. I never thought I'd see you again,' she said in a weak voice.

'It's so good to see you, Mama. I never thought we'd be together again either,' said Gabby, tears forming in her eyes.

Caitlan motioned for her daughter to help her to her feet.

'Mama, are you sure you're strong enough?'

'Yes dear, I want to see the animal that caused us all this pain.'

Gabby reluctantly helped her mother to the rear of the ambulance where they sat down on the bumper, legs dangling, nearly touching the ground. Caitlan stared long and hard at the evil heap of humanity crumpled against the wall.

'She's not much to look at, is she?' said Caitlan.

'No Mama, she's not much at all.'

Scafa, the cunning old vixen she had become over the years, was not quite done. Although she was sure her left arm was broken, she very slowly moved her right, lifting the wrist bracelet and pointed it toward the girl. Caitlan, even after all she'd been through, was the first to spot the movement.

'Gabby!'

The tone and alarm in her mother's voice caused Gabby to react within seconds. Before her giant wings could open, her sight and hearing were already fully developed, her knife-like nails reflecting off the midday sun.

As she looked over at Scafa she heard the *phut,t phutt, phutt* of the darts being fired. Gabby had never seen or heard of this kind of weapon but she didn't hesitate to react knowing nothing good could come from this woman.

The first one slammed into the door frame where it remained dripping its toxic cargo. Gabby pushed her mother backward into the ambulance as her transformation became complete.

Scafa looked up excitedly with both awe and incomprehension as the girl moved her right wing with dazzling speed, causing the second two darts to enter the mesh of feathers.

She checked her supply of darts for the mother, but glancing down even for a second was her final, fatal mistake. She had made the presumption that Gabby would not survive two darts but she had been wrong.

She lifted her head to see Gabriella, the girl she so desperately wanted to kill, standing over her. Gabby's wings were turning greyer and greyer, her jaw line stretching out, her hair brilliant white and her eyes, her eyes were blazing blood red.

She grabbed Scafa roughly by the hair, readied her talons for the kill, but was stopped by the scream of her mother.

'Gabby! No, darling. Please don't!' she pleaded.

It took her several seconds to realize it was not a stranger's voice. She continued to hold Scafa off the ground as she turned to look at her mother.

'Mother?' she asked.

'Please darling, no more death. Hasn't there been enough?' Caitlan said, teetering on weakened legs.

Before throwing the Romany up on the roof of the ambulance, Gabby cut off the bracelet with the sharpest claw of her index finger and then ran to support her mother. The genuine concern for helping Caitlan caused her wings to whiten once more upon touching her mother's arm.

'Are you strong enough for a journey mother?' she asked, helping her out of the vehicle.

'Yes, dear. I'll be fine. You won't kill her will you?' she asked once more pleadingly.

'No, Mama. I won't hurt her.'

Gabby set Caitlan down before walking to the rear doors. She slammed them shut, reattached the padlock, melting it to the steel hasp by the friction of two of her talons. She then leapt onto the roof and deftly cut a circle around the cowering gypsy. Scafa fell onto the floor below with a thud.

'You behave now.'

Then she re-welded the roof of the ambulance with the tips of her titanium wings, securing her arch-nemesis in the steel box, just like the assassins, Sheila and Philippe, had done to her weeks before.

'You'd better let in some air,' said Caitlan

Gabby looked at her mother remembering the compassion she had for all others around her. With five fingers of one hand she made air holes in the back door.

Gabby rooted through Scafa's handbag and pulled out the satellite phone. She examined it slowly before dialing 999, the number for the police force.

'Cleggan Garda Station please. Yes, Shanahan please. I'll wait. Tell him it's his friend who had to fly.' She looked at Caitlan and smiled.

'Garda Shanahan? Yes, it's Gabby. I need you to do me a favour. I have Scafa boxed up . . . where? Hold on a sec.'

Gabby, still holding the phone, launched herself skyward, checked for landmarks, then hovered back down landing on the exact spot she'd taken off from.

'The second turnoff after Shannonbridge, heading east. Yes, it's a deserted farm road. Yes, the ambulance is clearly visible. We'll be in the old farmhouse. Please come alone. Thank you.'

She hung up and sat down beside her mother.

'I'm so proud of you. It's the right thing to do, you know?' Caitlan said, as Gabby wrapped one huge wing around her.

Caitlan fingered the mass of feathers, some softer than others. Gabby suddenly remembered the darts and so laid out her other wing and started gently probing it with her talons. Two minutes later she had both darts removed. They'd never come close to penetrating her skin.

Half an hour later they heard the sirens approaching the lane. Gabby and her mother had hidden in the house where Gabby had recounted her adventures since the shooting at the campsite. They'd both cried in each other's arms at the memories of Caitlan's other children, Gabby's brothers and sister.

Back to being a girl, Gabby peeked out through the boarded up window and saw the Gardaí, some in uniform and some in suits, some with guns and some without, all milling around the ambulance.

'Is that the guards ? Shall we go to them?

'We wait, Mama. Shanahan is the only one I want to see.'

'But will they not help us?'

'The fewer people who see us, the better, Mama.'

Caitlan gazed at Gabby with so much pride and fascination of how much she'd grown into a woman since the shooting, that Gabby actually felt the emotion and turned from the window.

'Are you okay?' she asked smiling.

'Never better. Well actually, that's not quite true,' Caitlan said with a huge grin on her face.

Gabby laughed.

'But you're going to be fine, right?' asked Gabby.

'I'm already better, darling. Seeing you must be the reason.'

'I missed you so much. I was sure you were dead, Mama,' Gabby said, holding her mother's hand.

Caitlan looked deep into her daughters eyes and said,

'It's the strangest thing, sweetheart. The doctors told me the bullet that hit me actually seemed to change course on entry, missing my heart by millimeters.'

Gabby contemplated her mother's words for several seconds, remembering how the bullet had clipped her ear before striking Caitlan's chest. Hardly enough deflection to change the course of something travelling at 1,000 feet per second.

'Well that's bizarre, huh?' she said softly

'Indeed. Bizarre it is.'

Twenty minutes later they heard the sound of a helicopter landing close by. Not long after that there was a tapping sound on the corrugated hoarding across the front door.

'Gabby? Caitlan? It's Garda Sergeant Shanahan,' came a low voice.

Gabby leaned against the frame, talons poking out of her fingers, but not fully extended.

'Just being cautious,' she said to her mother.

'Coming in,' he said, pushing through the makeshift entry.

Gabby gave him an awkward hug.

'Sergeant? Well done! All because of me, right?' she said grinning.

'Yes. You were certainly a lot to do with it', he said, blushing slightly

Caitlan rose and accepted his handshake.

'Congratulations Sergeant,' she said sincerely.

'Thank you, Ma'am. How are you feeling?' he asked.

'Oh, I've been better, thank you,' she said, sitting once

more.

Before he could continue, a voice came over his radio.

'Sir, you'd better come look at this . . . '

'Wait here. Back in a sec,' he said, leaving the farmhouse.

Gabby went over to hold her mother.

'She couldn't have escaped, could she?' Caitlan asked.

'If she had a cutting torch in her shawl, maybe' said Gabby, trying to lighten the conversation.

A short while later Shanahan returned.

'After a cursory look, it appears Scafa is dead,' he said seriously.

'How can that be? I gave her air,' asked Gabby, feeling slightly uncomfortable.

'Oh, no. She had air. From the discolouration on her tongue, I'd say it was poison.'

'The dart. Remember it was dripping something, the one in the door frame,' Caitlan said, quickly.

Gabby nodded. The criminal mastermind of a worldwide dynasty would never want to be taken alive. It made sense to Gabby.

'Yes, I can see it. Failure was not an option,' said Gabby.

'Are we going to have to go to Dublin, Sergeant, to make a statement or something?' asked Caitlan, her voice weakening.

'Oh no, not necessary. I'll take care of all that.'

'So?' asked Gabby.

'So, I think we should all fly back to the island. Do you agree, Gabby?' he said.

Gabby looked at him up and down, then her mother.

'I don't think I can manage the two of you, but I could try,' she said in all sincerity.

'Why don't we take the helicopter? You're not the only one who can fly, you know?' he said, smiling.

'Deal,' she said. 'Nobody else coming, right?' Gabby asked, still thinking of their security.

'Just us three and no flight plan. I've cleared it with HQ' he said, proudly.

'Still, I'd like you to let us out somewhere other than where we're going, if you catch my meaning?' said Gabby.

'Absolutely, just let me know when and where,' Shanahan said leading them out of the door of the old farmhouse.

Gabby held onto her mother until they reached a clearing where a Vietnam-era Huey helicopter idled. It had *Garda* stamped on the side and looked big enough for ten people, no problem. Caitlan looked at her daughter in horror.

'Do you think it'll fly?' she asked.

'I hope so, but I've a backup plan, if it doesn't,' she said winking.

Once they were all installed, Shanahan took off smoothly heading north-west.

CHAPTER 39

With Jones, Mo Mo and Jane on their way back to the island, Binky was away from the house picking wild blackberries.

'Go away, you two,' said Binky, waving his free hand in the air.

Henry and Perdita were not any help at all. Binky was collecting berries for dinner. The two cockatoos were having theirs. After much shouting and gesticulating they flew off under the canopy.

'Peace, at last,' Binky said, turning back to the thicket, when suddenly it erupted. A large skin-blackened hand grabbed him by the throat. Binky fainted.

CJ tied up Marshy's lobster boat on the little dock before helping Jane and Mo Mo off.

'Ah, home again,' said Mo Mo.

'So peaceful . . . '

Jane was interrupted by the squealing of Henry and Perdita flying circles around them noisily.

'They're welcoming you home, isn't that grand?' said Jones, unaware of the thoughts of the women.

'Something's not right,' said Mo Mo. trying to catch Perdita.

'What's your problem, baby?' asked Jane of Henry, using the same tone her husband used to use with her.

'Something untoward dearest!' screeched Henry, bringing back memories of her poor, dead husband's love of the English language.

'What is it? Gabby, is it Gabby?' Crabapple Jones asked the bird, feeling a bit like an idiot.

'No Gabby! Fat boy's chicken is cooked, methinks!' screamed Henry.

'Oh no, Binky's in trouble, but how? You think there's more of these people?'

'Who knows? Shanahan and Binky said they blew up the monk but maybe they didn't. They never found his body,' Mo Mo whispered.

'He couldn't have swum all the way . . . could he . . . I suppose?'

'Is there a gun in the house?' CJ asked Mo Mo.

'There's an old hunting rifle above the fireplace, but I don't think it's been fired in years.'

'Hang on a sec. The one I fired at the trawler should still be on the boat.'

CJ turned and ran back down the hill, the two women close behind.

'We should call Cleggan and tell them what's going on,' Mo Mo said, as Jane picked up the ship to shore radio microphone.

'I'm going up there. You two stay here' said CJ, heading toward the house.

'Yes, it's Mo Mo Kelly on the island. Tell the police to send someone now. It's an emergency. What? We think there's someone holding our friend hostage . . . yes we think so. What? You'll be here when you can? What kind of . . .'

'Call Garda Mark Shanahan, please tell *him* what's going on, okay. Thank you,' Mo Mo said exasperated.

'Idiots!'

'Yes, Ma, I agree. What now?' said Mo Mo, finally

realizing Jones was heading up the path.

'I'm not staying here. CJ, hang on. You coming?'

'Hell, yes. I'm not staying here on my own.'

The intrepid threesome slowly marched toward the cottage, Jones leading the way, rifle in hand.

CHAPTER 40

Caitlan was stretched out dozing on her daughter's lap, wrapped in a blanket on the bench behind the cockpit. Shanahan was an accomplished pilot and the journey was uneventful. They talked little through the headphones. Gabby was exhausted and polite conversation held little appeal. That was until Shanahan got an emergency call from headquarters.

'Gabby! There's a situation on Kelly's Island.'

Gabby sat up suddenly on full alert nearly causing Caitlan to slip onto the floor.

'What is it?' asked mother and daughter in unison.

'From what I understand, it's possible Visnik, or one of his group, is alive and holding Binky captive,' he said, urgently.

Before he could say anything else, Gabby took over.

'How far from the island are we?'

Shanahan glanced at his flight control.

'Approximately fifteen miles, but . . ..

'But, nothing. I'm going alone. You take Mama and land in Clifden. Stay with her, Sergeant. Please take care of her,' she said, hugging her mother before sliding open the door and leaping out of the speeding helicopter.

'Gabby. No no! Oh God, Gabby, be careful!' screamed Caitlan, as Shanahan reached behind him closing the door.

He banked the helicopter, both peering out for any sign of Gabby but all they saw was her ripped T shirt spiralling downward.

Visnik slapped Binky a couple of times, relieved the fat man wasn't dead. *Dead was no good to him yet*, he thought to himself allowing a hint of a smile to cross his face. He took hold of one of Binky's legs and pulled him unceremoniously out of the thicket.

When Binky came to, he was blindfolded, tied to a chair somewhere outside. He could feel the springy ground beneath his feet. He had a rag in his mouth and there was a smell of old canvas invading his nostrils. There was something else too, but at first he couldn't place it.

'It's the mad monk,' he said to himself, recognizing the putrid stench of bad breath, petrol and charred flesh all assaulting his senses at the same time. He could also feel the cold steel of a gun barrel pressed firmly against his neck.

Jones, Mo Mo and Jane arrived at the clearing in front of the house a few minutes later. Inside the house Jack was howling like a dog possessed. Henry and Perdita were screeching sounds of alarm.

They all stopped, trying to work out what exactly they were looking at in the front garden.

'Was someone camping?' asked Mo Mo, peering closer.

She saw slash marks in the canvas and what looked like a pair of feet sticking out from underneath the dark green bundle.

'What in the world . . .?' interrupted Jane

'Throw down your weapon, boy!' came Visnik's rasping voice.

Jones naturally raised the gun, pointing it toward the bulbous mass, not sure what to do.

'Wait! Where's Binky?' shouted Mo Mo, moving in front of Jones.

Under the canvas ,Visnik roughly pulled out the gag and prodded Binky in the kidneys with his curved dagger while resting the rifle on his shoulder.

'Say something . . . Binky,' said Visnik, peering out through one of the slashes he'd made earlier.

'Shoot! Shoot us! Shoot!' screamed the little fat man before Visnik replaced the gag and put the knife to his neck.

'That's enough, little man.'

Jones nudged Mo Mo aside, aiming the rifle once more. Before either of the women could stop him, a shot rang out and CJ dropped to the ground squirming in pain.

Jane knelt down beside him and checked the shoulder wound.

'Leave him! If you don't listen to me, you'll both be next.'

'But he could die,' screamed Jane.

Visnik laughed saying, 'We all have to die, some sooner than others. Pull the boy closer to me, now!'

The two women had little choice and so as gently as they could, they moved him closer to the monk's tent.

Jones was unconscious.

'Now tell me this. Does anyone know when the girl, Gabriella, is returning? If you don't answer me truthfully, I will have to shoot one of you, which may well ruin your future plans. Ha ha.'

Jane and Mo Mo looked at each other, hopelessly, knowing whatever they said it really wouldn't change what the crazed man was ultimately going to do.

'We won't tell you. You'll just shoot us, anyway,' screamed Mo Mo.

Another shot rang out as Mo Mo clutched her knee.

'You are proud but stupid, all of you. Just tell me where . . .'

Gabby had landed a minute earlier on the U-shaped branch of the tallest fir tree, five hundred yards from the cottage. She had watched in horror as Jones was shot in the shoulder and was formulating a plan when suddenly she saw Mo Mo being shot also.

The crazy monk was concealing himself well under the canvas, picking them off until she made her move. She had no alternative now, she decided.

Because his view was limited, Gabby landed on the roof of the canopy not far above where the four were being held. She carefully sliced open a hole with her right hand index talon. She pulled back the section of photo voltaic cells and peered down.

His idea was correct, in principle, she thought.

Don't let her see me and she won't dare attack for fear of causing the death of Binky.

'Boy, do you have that wrong!' she whispered to herself, folding her wings in and then dropping like a stone toward her cautious foe.

As Gabby opened her magnificent white wings, she let out an incredibly high-pitched scream causing all who could to cover their ears for fear their drums would perforate.

Binky was pretty sure he knew what caused this screeching wail and so by shifting his body weight he caused the chair to topple to the ground. This left Visnik a taller target than he had planned for.

Gabby swept down from the top of the canopy landing full force on Visnik's chest, shredding the canvas with her slashing feet talons and then lifted him up above her shoulders.

Visnik stared into her eyes with such animosity and hatred, it seemed he was trying to will her to surrender or die.

Neither worked.

So he did the next best thing. He pulled out his shortened Scimitar-like knife and slashed it across her throat. Like a man possessed he began to laugh and laugh at what he'd done, thinking she would undoubtedly release him to stem the flow of blood.

But there was no flow of blood, in fact there was no blood at all.

Binky, Mo Mo, Jane and CJ were transfixed by what happened next. Gabby's eyes glazed over with a protective membrane, her pupils deep yellow, the sclera bright red. Her jawline jutted down and her hair changed to white. But her wings didn't stay white for long. They got darker and darker until they were black, all except for the long underside end feathers. They turned a brilliant red.

She lifted a now terrified Visnik over her head and with giant wings beating furiously carried him off out over the sea.

Jane untied Binky and they both tended to the two shooting victims. Neither was gravely injured. They all watched with morbid curiosity as Gabby stopped and hovered thousands of feet above the ocean.

She lowered Visnik to eye level as her large black and red wings beat methodically. Her eye membrane retracted as she calmed slightly to study the man who had caused so much pain.

'You're an evil man you know.'

'This I know. But I promise you, if you let me go I will cancel all contracts on you and your family.'

Gabby studied him for second.

'You'd do that for me?'

'Yes, yes, of course.'

'Okay,' she said and let him go.

The group on the island said he screamed all the way down before connecting with the sea. Nobody could survive that fall. Gabby's wings slowly changed back to all white, her eyes back to green and even her hair began changing back to red although she was still flying.

As she landed she started to return to normal once more. Jane removed her own shawl and wrapped it around Gabby's shoulders. The whole episode had shaken Gabby to the core. She never imagined the strength she could achieve, or how terrifying she could become.

Jack and even little Sophie came out of the house after being freed by Binky. Henry and Perdita, well, they acted like cockatoos do.

Gabby checked on Mo Mo's knee first, quickly deciding she might need a bit of surgery. Moving on, she held CJ in her arms while examining the wound. She smiled, released two of her talons and started rubbing them together. They began to glow red. He shrieked, as smoke began to rise,

'I can take care of this. Be brave,' she said, in all seriousness.

'No, no. Stop. It's okay, I can wait,' he shrieked, really unsure if she was going to burn him.

Still with a straight face, Gabby said,

'Sure it won't hurt that much. Are you a baby or what?'

'Yes, that's it. I'm a baby,' he said, nervously.

She gave him a huge grin as her talons cooled and retracted.

'You're my baby then,' she said leaning forward and kissed him long and hard on the lips.

Shanahan and Caitlan landed in the helicopter a few minutes later and there was a tremendous reunion. After much laughter and tears, Shanahan decided it would be best to take Mo Mo and CJ off to the hospital in Clifden for a little repair work. Gabby helped her mother up the stairs and into the bedroom next door to hers. Binky and Jane tidied up the garden area and then sat down on the couch in front of the fire. They talked about their lives and how both had lost a spouse at relatively young ages.

Gabby lay across Caitlan's big bed, both stroking and petting Sophie who purred like a sewing machine.

'Well, I hope that's the end of it,' Caitlan said.

'Me too,' was all Gabby replied staring out of the roof at the birds, the trees, the beauty and wonders of nature.

'What is to become of me?' she asked herself.

. . . .END . . . .

ABOUT THE AUTHOR

Alan was born in 1955 in Dublin, Ireland. He has lived and worked in the UK, France and Venice, California before finally settling in Connemara on the west coast of Ireland. He finds his inspiration in the wild landscape of mountains and windswept seas off the Atlantic coast.